# Enchanted Legends and Lore of New Mexico

# Enchanted Legends and Lore of New Mexico

*Witches, Ghosts & Spirits*

Ray John de Aragón

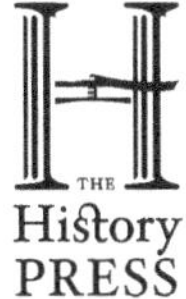

Published by The History Press
Charleston, SC 29403
www.historypress.net



First published 2012

Manufactured in the United States

ISBN 978.1.60949.572.5

Library of Congress Cataloging-in-Publication Data

De Aragon, Ray John.
Enchanted legends & lore of New Mexico : witches, ghosts and holy spirits / Ray John de Aragon.
p. cm.
ISBN 978-1-60949-572-5
1. Folklore--New Mexico. 2. Legends--New Mexico. 3. Tales--New Mexico. 4. Hispanic Americans--New Mexico--Folklore. 5. Witches--New Mexico--Anecdotes. 6. Ghosts--New Mexico--Anecdotes. 7. Apparitions--New Mexico--Anecdotes. 8. New Mexico--Social life and customs--Anecdotes. I. Title.
GR110.N6D4 2012
398.209789--dc23
2012005896

# CONTENTS

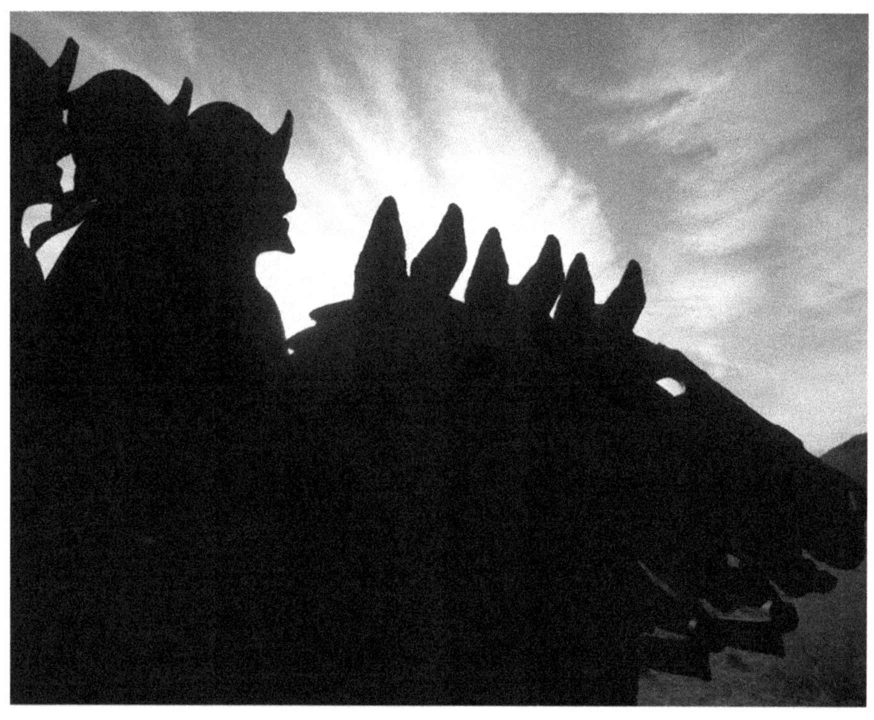

"La Entrada," photograph. *©2010 Ramon Juan Carlos de Aragón. Courtesy of the author.*

# THE DEDICATION

In 1598, our Spanish ancestors—fathers, mothers and their children—arrived to colonize New Mexico to start a new life. Along with their dreams for the future, these Spanish families introduced their faith and a rich ancient heritage and culture from Spain and changed the New Mexican landscape forever, leaving us with a precious legacy.

With the founding of the capital city of La Villa Real de la Santa Fé de San Francisco de Asís in 1610, these intrepid pioneers ensured for their descendants that the impact of their traditions would continue through the centuries. The marvelous Spanish culture they transplanted and nourished to grow included the beauty of Penitente spiritual life, the strength of the architecture, the power of the art and music and the magical wonder of the folklore and legends.

I dedicate this book with heartfelt devotion to Nuevo México, and especially to my family: Rosa María Calles, Rosalía, Lucía, Ramón, Linda, Enrique, Omri, Santiago, Estevan, Rosalinda and Francisco. I also appreciate the assistance that Marisa Rodriguez de Aragón provided. My wife, Rosa, with her marvelous skills as an established and widely recognized artist, producer, director and playwright, as my partner, supporter and advisor provided her talents to help realize the completion of this work. I sincerely dedicate this book to her encouragement and devotion to my efforts. With each succeeding generation, our courageous grandfather and grandmother forbearers passed down a torch that still burns brightly and enflames our very souls and our very beings with a glorious and vibrant history.

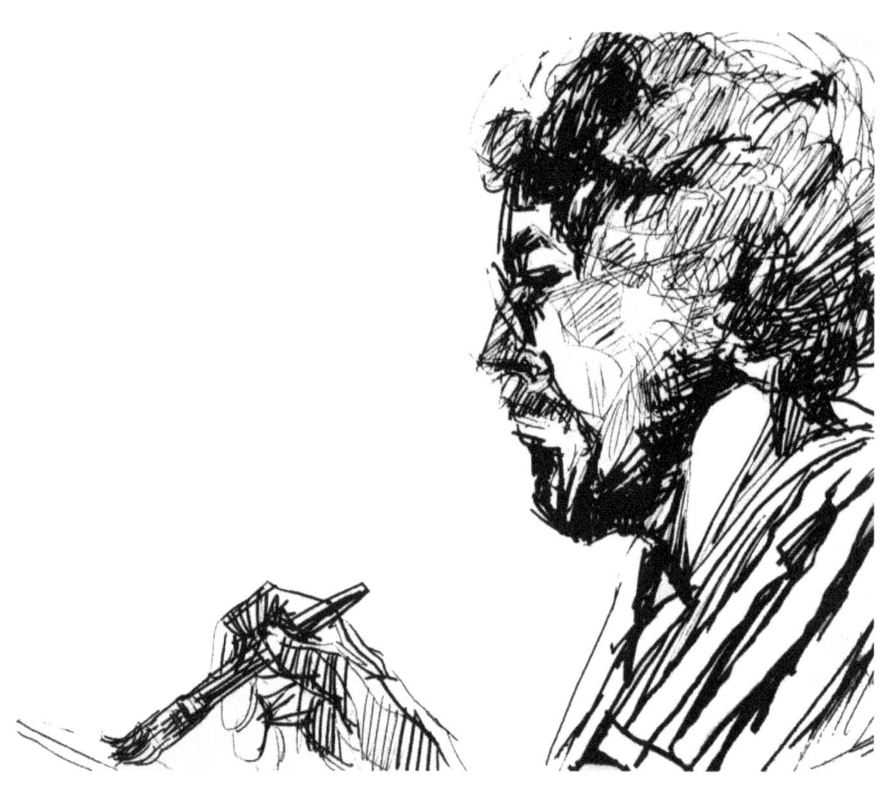

Pen-and-ink drawing of Ray John de Aragón by Mie Shu Ou. *Courtesy of the author.*

# "THE BOOK"

*One day I found a book*
*buried deep within my mind.*
*I read the pages of the dreams*
*that were at one time left behind.*
*Memories of things long gone*
*suddenly came alive.*
*Some were pleasant,*
*others nightmares that I would not dare contrive.*
*This book was filled with ghosts and specters,*
*darkened shadows of the night.*
*And I tried to block each one*
*with my strength and all my might.*
*But no matter how I tried,*
*they came back and once again,*
*I read it and reread it*
*and this is how it all began…*

# FORWARD INTO THE UNKNOWN

*El miedo; las cosas que no son nos hacen padecer,*
*y las cosas que son, no parecen ser.*

Fear; things that are not make us suffer,
and things that are we don't believe.

In my family, like in other New Mexico Hispano families, recollections of people and events were always passed down through oral history. It was always left to the Old Ones to relate what they knew, had heard or remembered about what everyone considered important in the villages or towns. It was my mother, María Cleofas Sánchez de Aragón, who came from the valley of Peñasco Blanco near Mora, who taught me to be proud of our New Mexican Spanish heritage, which included our stories and legends.

The old stories of New Mexico always had a lesson that was taught. The moral endings were meant to change lives and to help people appreciate things. *Cuentos* (stories) brought from Spain by the early settlers in the sixteenth century included the tale of *La Llorona* (the Wailing Woman) and the legend of *El Koko*, the boogeyman of the dark. I grew up with La Llorona and El Koko in Las Vegas, New Mexico, where our family, relatives and neighbors had a firm belief in witches, ghosts and holy spirits. The interesting thing back in those days was that people always pointed out where a ghost had been seen, where La Llorona lived or where witches hung around. The title *difunto* or *difunta* was used before a first name to let listeners know that the person

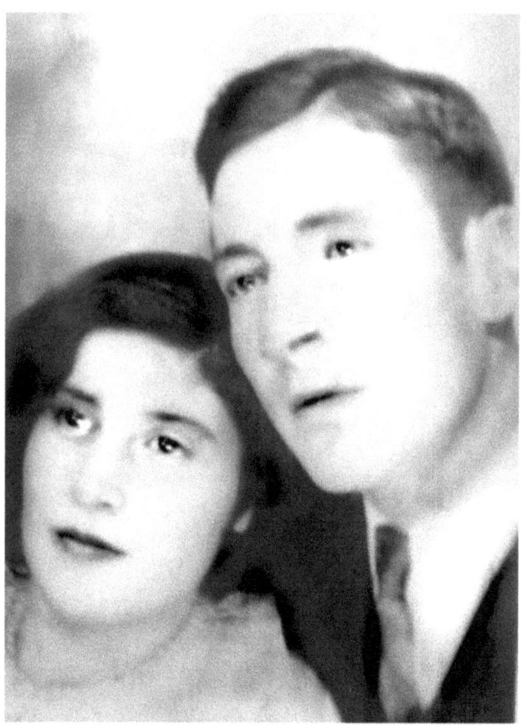

*Left*: Maximo de Aragón and María Cleofas Sanchez de Aragón. *Courtesy of the author.*

*Below*: Rosalia de Aragón portrays La Llorona, a popular New Mexico Spanish legend about a spirit that haunts the waterways searching for her children. *©2001 Rosa María Calles.*

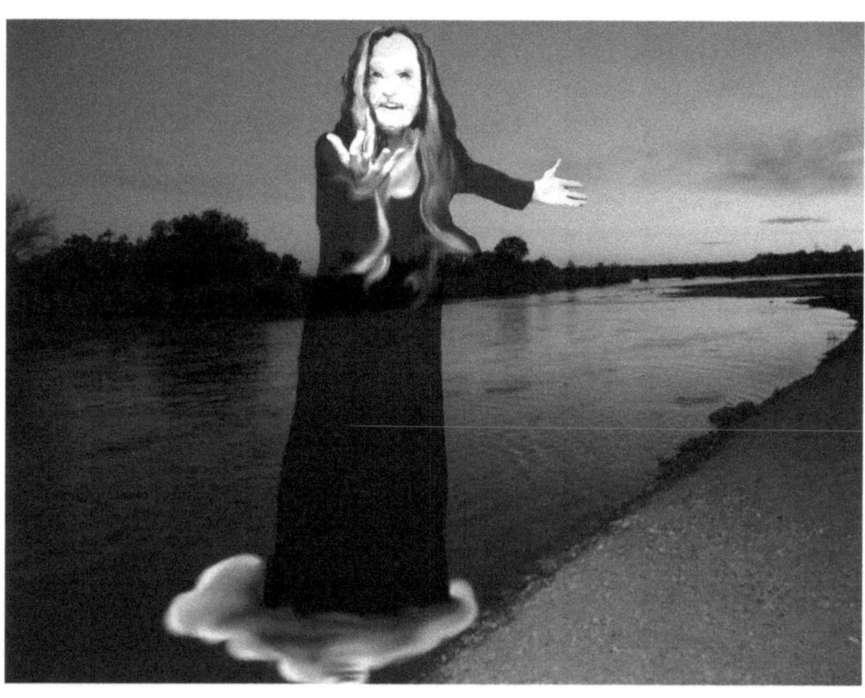

about whom they were speaking had died. People loved to share stories, and I spent many days and nights sitting in the kitchen as a young boy near a wood stove, cracking and eating *piñon* nuts or eating *tortillas*, beans, red or green *chile*, *empanaditas* and *bizcochitos* while I enthusiastically listened to my mother as she recalled stories from the past. At one time or another, all of us in the family had an experience that could not be explained.

One of my uncles had crucifixes all over his house. He was a member of the Penitente Brotherhood and was always at church. My grandfather, who lived next door to him and who was an elder member of the brotherhood, was always praying. I liked visiting my uncle and aunt, not only for their stories, but also because my uncle had been a furniture maker under the WPA. This was the Works Progress Administration established by President Franklin D. Roosevelt to provide work for thousands of unemployed people during the Great Depression in the 1930s. The government funded an arts program, which had an artists' division. My uncle was one of those artists. He made pine wood furniture in the early Spanish colonial style of New Mexico, and his house was full of what he created. He and my other uncles had made coffins in the community of Peñasco Blanco when they were younger. My uncle called the WPA *El Diablo a Pie*, which means the "Devil on Foot." This was just a way of turning the English abbreviation into a Spanish phrase that all of the natives understood. Each coffin my uncles built was a work of art.

The Spanish colonial heritage of New Mexico revolved around oral history, the Catholic faith and Spanish culture and tradition. The early Spanish *dicho* (proverb) *El temor siempre sospecha lo peor* (Fear always leads us to suspect the worst) helped people to be wary and careful. This coincided with a natural fear of the unknown and mysterious happenings that could not be explained. These commonly held mysteries included the belief that the chilling cries of cats or owls late at night served as emissaries of death and that someone would die soon after. It was also believed that the souls of the living—moments, hours or even days before death—could travel to places the person wanted to see one last time or visit people to give their farewells. These *almas agonizando* (agonizing souls), as they were called in New Mexico, presumably had the pre-death freedom to roam and go anywhere they wanted before they left on their final journey. The Old Ones say this was in sharp contrast to *almas que andan penando* (souls in search of peace).

Everyone knows about shadows that follow you or those invisible beings that watch you. I loved all of the unearthly folk stories of New Mexico. The comings and goings of ghosts attracted my attention. Witches traversing the night were as real to me as sunshine and moonlight, but it was the sounds of night, like the distant howl of a *coyote* or the hoot of an owl, and the strange compelling allure of the dark that attracted me the most. Herein I record what I heard and learned.

*I*

# HISTORICAL OVERVIEW

## *Witches*

| | |
|---|---|
| *Oh, Ángel Guardián protégeme* | Oh, Guardian Angel protect me |
| *de todo malhechor,* | from all wrongdoers |
| *guíame al reino celestial,* | guide me to heaven, |
| *cuídame encontra hechizos,* | guard me from spells and |
| *y de espíritus malos sálvame.* | save me from evil spirits. |
| | |
| *Cura para hechizos:* | A cure for spells: |
| *una rosa de canela,* | a rose of cinnamon, |
| *una cebolla morada,* | a purple onion, |
| *una cabeza de ajo,* | a head of garlic, |
| *uno al horado,* | one every hour, |
| *miel en oropel.* | honey in a plate of brass. |

During the sixteenth through eighteenth centuries, the belief in witches and wizards was widespread throughout Europe. It was thought that some people possessed special magical powers. In some cases, these individuals could become invisible, or they could transform themselves into animals and even fly. This idea was also prevalent in New Mexico among the Spanish colonists. Some of the earliest cases of people being *embrujados* or bewitched by wizards and witches in New Mexico come from 1631.

Fray Esteban de Perea, who served as a representative of the Inquisition in New Mexico from 1631 to 1639, constantly reported his investigations back to the central government of New Spain, detailing his discoveries in

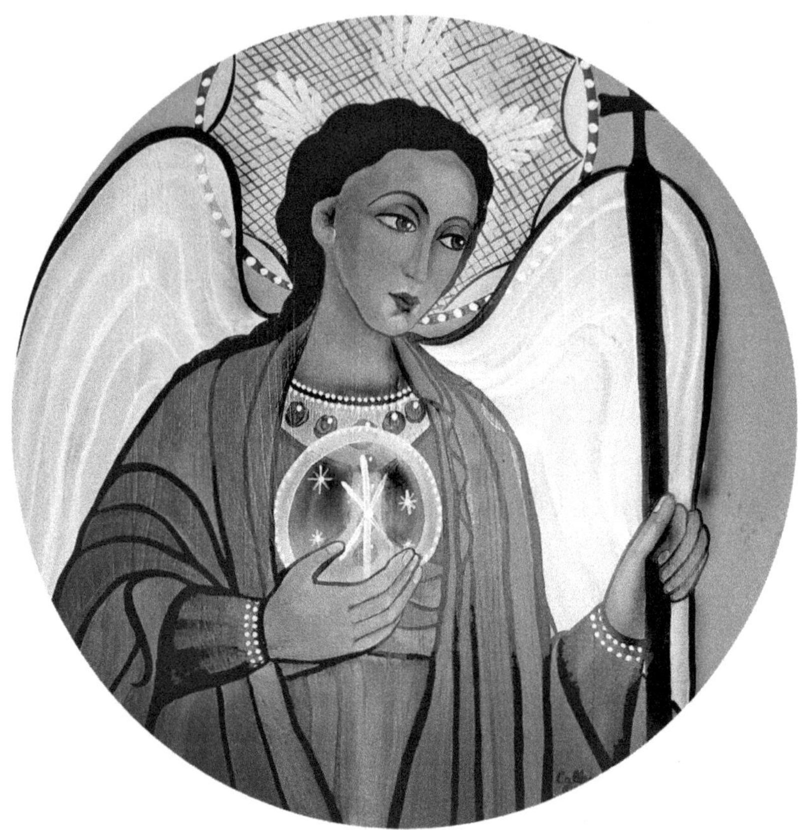

*Guardian Angel*, retablo. *©2010 Rosa María Calles.*

Santa Fé and the surrounding areas. According to the *fray*, the use of love potions was rapidly spreading. He said the colonists used fried worms and urine concocted in potions given to them by witches. They also used *peyote*, a hallucinogenic drug, which was given to them by Indian witch doctors. Since the Indians were exempt by Spanish law from the Inquisition, it appears that they freely sold purportedly magical potions to the Spanish. The *fray* also claimed that witches in New Mexico could travel from one place to another in eggs that mysteriously floated in the air. Investigations and witch hunts started with fervor as a result of the fray's reports.

In one case, some women from Santa Fé were charged with witchery. Beatriz de los Angeles and her daughter, Juana de la Cruz, supposedly gave a potion to a Juan Bellido that made him deathly ill. Even the governor, Sotelo Osorio, got involved and sent for a witch from San Juan Pueblo to try to cure

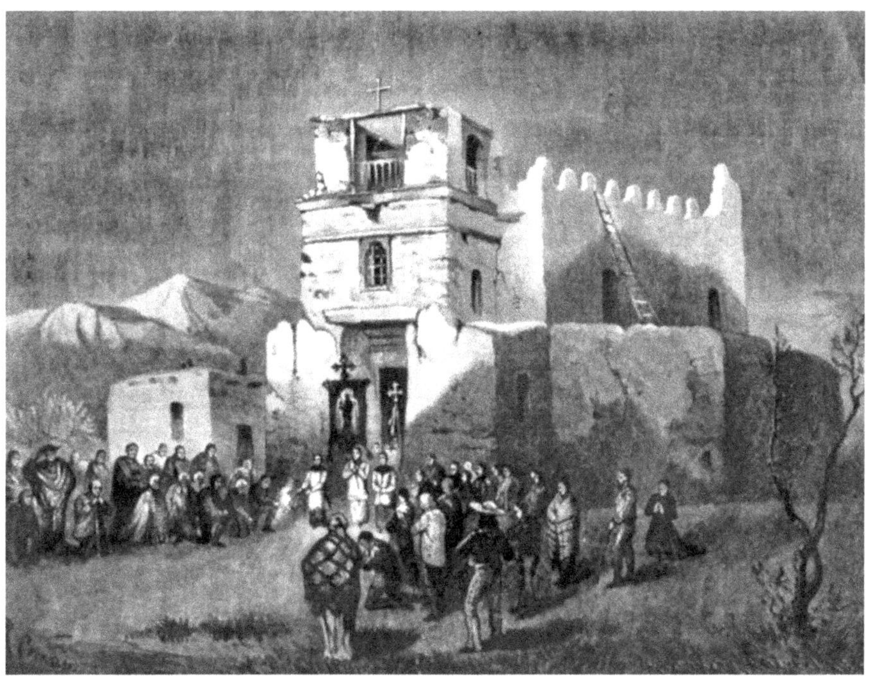

*Die Stiedie San Miguel, Santa Fe, Originalzeidmung von Rudolf Cronau*, circa 1830. *Author's collection.*

him, but Bellido died. The woman and her daughter were charged with practicing witchcraft, and it seems that in one way or another they were said to have been involved in several other mysterious deaths. Interestingly, Fray de Perea wound up dismissing all of the charges against the two women.

In another case, a German named Bernard Gruber and a colonist named Juan Serrano were accused of practicing talismanic magic at the *pueblo* of Quarai in 1668. They were accused of being wizards who were conjuring up black magic along with sorcerers of the Tewa pueblos. While trying to escape trial, they were both killed by the Apaches near Socorro, New Mexico.

Governor Juan Francisco Treviño acted on reports of witchcraft in 1675. Forty-seven Indians, some of whom were from San Felipe, Jémez and Nambé, were arrested and taken to Santa Fé. They were charged with bewitching Fray Andrés Duran from San Ildefonso and three other Spaniards, plus killing seven frays. Four of the Indians were found guilty and hanged, and the others were severely punished. Captain Francisco Javier of the Santa Fé presidio had gone along with a contingent of soldiers, gathering up incriminating evidence that included charms, fetishes and powders. The testimony, along with the evidence, was supposed to have been overwhelming.

In 1703, Antonia Moraga of Chimayo was taken to a hearing before Inquisition authorities in Santa Fé. She was accused of taking part in some occult ceremonies to practice *maleficio* (witchcraft). Her husband, Felipe Moraga, claimed that his wife had conspired with three San Juan Pueblo witches to perform magic to make him blind. He said he had been forced to get the services of a more powerful San Juan witch to perform curing rites to save his eyesight. After hearing both sides, the inquisitors decided to take no action.

In Abiquiú in 1760, several deaths induced by witchcraft were said to have occurred. Fray Juan José de Toledo sent a dispatch to the governor, Don Francisco Marín del Valle, informing him about the veneration of the devil around the area in order to secure his help in injuring or captivating others. Accusers said love potions were freely used, and the witches gave various powers to certain people. These people were also given the ability to fly. De Toledo pointed out what specific things investigators should look for while searching for real sorcerers.

During this same period, a young girl named Paula accused Vicente Trujillo and his wife, María de la Candelabra, of goading her into unholy deeds with animals and teaching her about spells. She said they took her to a cave in El Cerro del Pedernal and ordered her to remove a cross on a chain from her neck. Then she had to kiss a toad in the cave that turned into a man, who joined them. She was told to kiss another animal, but she instead asked for help from *La Santisíma Trinidad* (the Holy Trinity). She was then severely warned and forced to watch the husband and wife do their magic, which included changing into animals from the waist up but remaining human from the waist down.

Many interesting things came out of the witch trials of early New Mexico. It was determined that some purported witches used spoiled *cuajadas*, the curd of milk separated from the whey, which they gave to unsuspecting victims to cause illness or even death. The clear, straw-colored liquid was sometimes mixed with powders to create an evil potion. The frays believed that something from the dark side was pulling these people to do things they would not otherwise do. Isabel la Pastora was said to be a witch who liked to perform her magic undressed from the waist up, especially when she did the *Baile de las Tortugas*, the Dance of the Turtles. Other witches—like La Fabiana, who was described as middle aged and exceedingly dark and ugly, La Chana and La Agua Fría—were all said to have used fingernails, teeth, molars, hair and the bones of the dead, along with powders and poisonous plants, in their concoctions. Sometimes when a Spanish female had fantastic intuition or was extremely intelligent, she was accused of being the mistress of the devil, the Incarnate Evil One. Some of the people who were suspected of witchcraft and sorcery were shackled and placed for a period in wooden stocks at Santa Fé. Others received warnings and lashings if they repented and then were eventually released.

Fortunately, people back in those days believed they had many things at their disposal to protect them against evil in the world. Bells were placed around the necks of cows and sheep to chase away evil spirits. The sound of ringing bells was thought to make flying witches crash into the ground. People in New Mexico were afraid of witches because they believed they were very powerful, but they also thought the witches could be foiled by a good trick. Outsmarting a witch was the basis of many good old stories. The stories told about witches in New Mexico were not always filled with hell, fire and brimstone. Stories such as "The Bruja's Curse" and "Crisscrossed Witches" were pretty lighthearted, while others—like "Los Voladeros/The Flyers," "The Headless Horseman of Santa Fé" and "Fearless John/Juan Sin Miedo"—are meant to warn people to beware of magic, enchantment or evil spells.

## The Bruja's Curse

*El que el mal busca, mal halla.*
One, who seeks evil, finds it.

One day, a middle-aged woman named Josefa stepped out of her modest but comfortable little adobe house. She began to visit with one of her neighbors down the road who was tending to her pungent *chile* plants. The plants were packed with the taste-tempting but hot deep-green fruits. Josefa and her very old neighbor had much to talk about. They both loved gossip, and they were never without a subject to discuss. Josefa had heard strange rumors about her good neighbor but didn't think they could be true, so she just kept on enjoying her neighbor's company. Unfortunately, the rumors were true. It turned out that the neighbor was an old *bruja*, a witch.

One day, Josefa appeared a little troubled. "What is the matter?" her neighbor asked.

Josefa explained why she had a heavy heart: "I haven't seen my son since he went to work sheepherding in the far north. It has been three months since he left. Manuel promised he would write at least once a month to let me know how he was getting along. I've been so worried that something may have happened to him. What should I do?"

The bruja couldn't bear to see her only friend so unhappy, so she came up with a plan to help her. "There is a way that you can find out if your son is well and safe, but you must swear that you will not reveal the secret way that I will show you, or harm may come to you."

Josefa was close to despair, so at this point she would have agreed to anything. At first she was puzzled, but then she decided. "I swear it. I will not reveal anything. You can confide in me. I won't speak to a soul about this."

"OK, then," the bruja said. "Meet me at my house at the stroke of midnight, and be prepared for a surprise."

The poor woman was there on time. "My, my, you are quite punctual," the bruja said with a smile. "That is a good sign."

Josefa was led into a dimly lit room. The room was empty except for a washtub on the floor, which was placed in the middle of the room. The tub was covered with a white sheet. Josefa was instructed to sit cross-legged next to the tub while the bruja stooped down across from her and placed her hands lightly over the sheet. Suddenly, she pulled the sheet back while mumbling some strange words Josefa could not understand. In the shimmering water that filled the tub, Josefa could see her son reflected as clear as day. He was having a great time talking with his friends, singing and drinking *capulin* wine. Josefa had no idea how the old woman had done it, but she felt as though a heavy burden had been lifted from her heart. She thanked her old friend and went happily home.

A few weeks later, Josefa unexpectedly bumped into her friend Alicia while shopping in Las Vegas. It turned out that Alicia had her own problems. She confessed that her husband, Rudolfo, had gone sheepherding with the others, and she hadn't heard a thing from him in nearly five months. "Josefa," she cried, "I don't know what to do anymore! I don't know where Rudolfo is or what has happened to him. How is it that you stay so calm? Don't you worry about your son?"

Josefa responded, "My son is doing just fine."

Alicia quickly asked, "Has he written? Did he mention my husband? Are they alright?"

Alicia remembered the old woman's warning, but she knew what Alicia was going through. "I know of someone who may be able to help you, but you mustn't tell her who told you about her. You must promise!"

Alicia wholeheartedly agreed, so Josefa explained about her own experience and gave her friend the directions to the old lady's home. Alicia

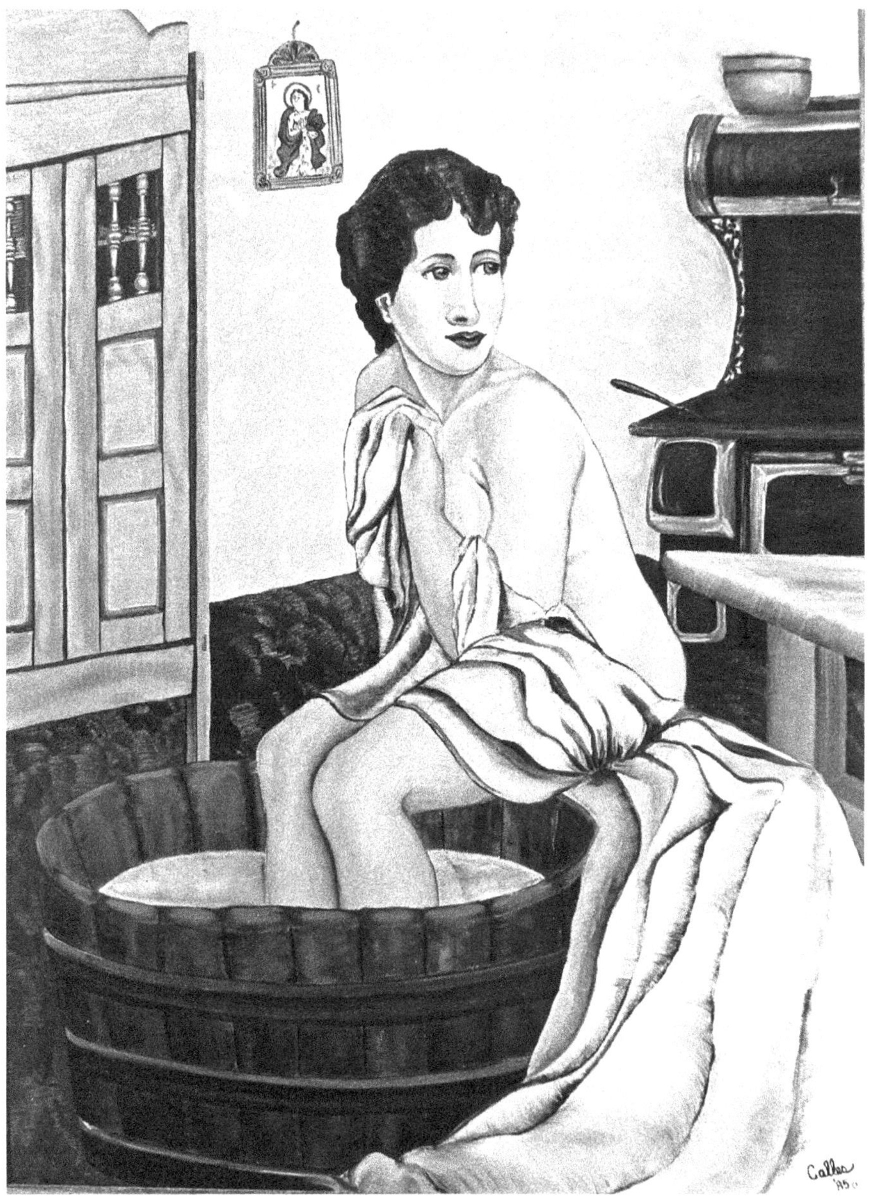

*El Baño*, oil on canvas. *©1989 Rosa María Calles. Courtesy Ray Salazar collection.*

was so anxious to know about her husband that she went to the bruja's house that very night. She knocked on the door, but no one was there. The door suddenly opened. Alicia walked in searching for the old lady. She found the room where the unusual tub was kept. Recalling what her friend had told her, Alicia sat cross-legged in front of the tub. Seeing the sheet, she pulled it off. At first she saw only water, but then her husband was slowly revealed to her eyes. A look of surprise quickly turned into one of shock. There was Rudolfo without a stitch of clothing, and there near him was another woman as naked as a jaybird. Alicia ran out of the house. She was so upset that she didn't notice the bruja approaching her home from a trip out to the *llano* (plain).

When the bruja saw Alicia, she wondered if Josefa had broken her promise. Of course, Alicia and others in the community were always trying to find out what she was up to. Alicia could have searched her home and found something that really upset her. But Josefa wouldn't break her promise, the bruja thought. She was a loyal friend. Days passed, and Alicia's anger became vicious. She spread rumors throughout the town that Josefa and her elderly friend were witches. Alicia alleged that the witches had cast spells on the men of the village who were gone sheepherding to make them do things they would not have done otherwise. The rumors became more and more fantastic as they spread around the town.

The witch, upon hearing these stories, decided that the village women should pay for their lies. She went into the room with the tub and raised her crooked cane over the water, which began to move in a circle. The water began to spin, and soon the water rose up and the witch's feet came off the floor. She chanted, "May those who have looked into this water or revealed its secrets have their tongues turned into knots, and may they suffer excruciating pain when they spread their lies." The story goes that every time the women attempted to spread rumors about the old woman and Josefa, their tongues would twist and turn and cause such pain that they would stay quiet. The villagers learned that if they didn't have anything nice to say about people, they shouldn't say anything at all.

The good old witch, with a smile on her face, would ask Josefa questions about her tub with the magic water. The witch knew that it was Josefa who had let her secret out, but only because she was concerned about her friend Alicia. Josefa understood that her blameless old friend had trusted her with a secret, and by sharing that secret with Alicia, she had betrayed her. So if her old friend wanted to tease her now and then with questions about the magic water, knowing that she could not answer since she, too, had been touched by the curse, it was OK.

Josefa and the witch remained loyal and worthy friends. Soon, the men returned to the village and were quite surprised at the silence of the women in their homes. Rudolfo never returned home. The women knew why, but they never told their tale. The men knew also, but they weren't about to tell his story to anyone. They thought, "There but for the grace of God go I. Why stir up the waters?"

## Los Voladeros/The Flyers

*Con cuidado se evita la brasa.*
Forewarned is forearmed.

Way back over a hundred years ago, a story began about a man named Buenaventura Angel. The man liked his last name, Angel, because he thought the angels protected him. Angel heard stories about a hidden village called Los Voladeros that was up in the clouds surrounded by mountains at the highest point near Mora. He and his friends were told never to go there. He knew it was a very mysterious place. It was an area where anyone could be charmed completely and fascinated to the point of ecstasy and then death. Since things were very boring and humdrum where he lived, and some people think they are invincible, Angel decided to check this place out. He wondered what could be at Los Voladeros that could captivate someone and enchant him or her to the point of death. Angel didn't believe that was possible. After all, the old people talked about it, but no one could name anyone who had actually died by going there. He thought they were just stories to keep people home and away from adventure.

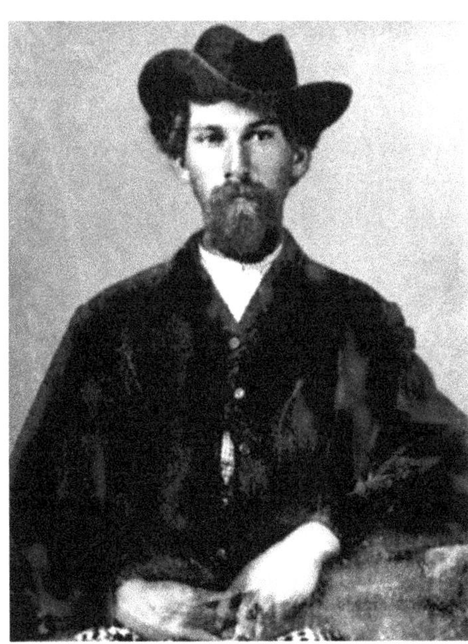

Tintype photograph, circa 1870s. *Author's collection.*

Angel loaded up his horse with provisions and headed toward Los Voladeros. He wanted to experience new things. He was tired of the old ways. Angel had started out at the crack of dawn that day, but by the time he got

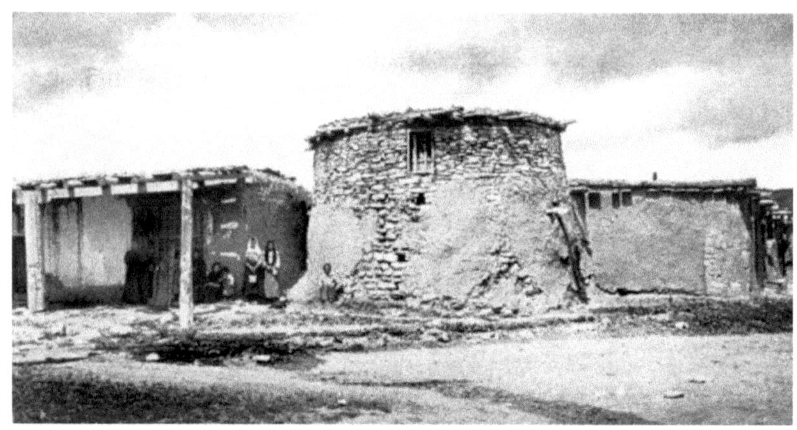

Torreon, photo tint card, Detroit Publishing Co., circa 1908. *Author's collection.*

near the crest of the mountain, it was dark. Angel had been warned that if he arrived after dark he was to walk slowly through a narrow path lighted by the full moon. He was not to stray away from the path or he would never get out alive. He would know when he had reached the hidden village by the hoot of many owls.

After following a trail, which went through tall pine trees and brush, Angel spotted *chispas* (sparks) rising into the crisp night sky from chimneys. The chispas and the hoots of owls led him to the village. He snuck up to a fortress-like wall, found an opening and got in. No sooner was he in the strange village than he fell to the ground unconscious. He was captured and thrown into a *torreon*, a circular adobe tower that had been used by early setters as protection against attacking, marauding Indians.

In the morning, Angel woke up to the smell of a breathtakingly delicious breakfast of *atole*, made with blue cornmeal, honey and milk, and *pastelitos*, little thin square pies filled with fruit. He was a prisoner, but he could not resist the delectable meal. He ate so much that he could not keep from sleeping once again when he was done. Angel woke up a second time to find the most beautiful girl his eyes could ever imagine standing in front of him. Angel immediately fell madly in love with this girl, whom he learned was named Dulubina.

One day, Angel got to meet Dulubina's mother, Doña Calada. Her mother was also very pleasing. Eventually, Angel was let out of the torreon. As he walked around the village, he thought it curious that he only saw beautiful women of different ages walking around with long black dresses and long black, frilled shawls. He wondered where the men of the village were. After a

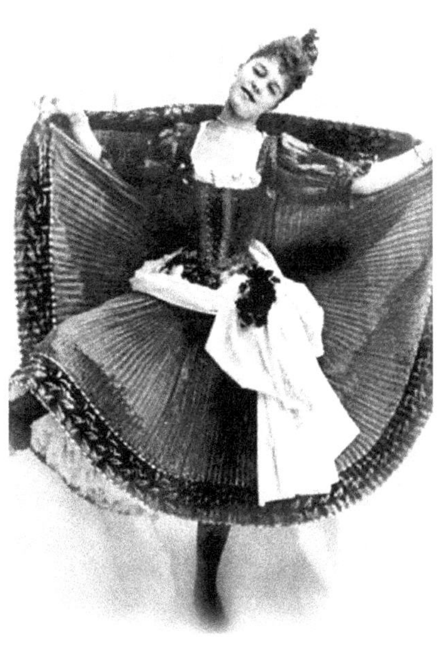
Carte de visite, circa 1870. *Author's collection.*

few days, he didn't give it much more thought. He was totally enchanted by the lovely Dulubina.

One day, Angel asked Dulubina to marry him. Even he was surprised by his own sudden inclination toward marriage since he was a confirmed bachelor. He realized he didn't know much about Dulubina, and yet he was delighted when she agreed to marry him. Dulubina wore a beautiful black dress, black lace gloves and a black shawl that had embroidered black roses on it for their wedding. Angel wondered why his betrothed would wear black instead of the traditional white for their wedding. But she was such a striking beauty with flaming red lipstick, red cheeks and red roses in her dark hair and pinned to the shawl that she mesmerized him beyond belief. Even her mysterious eyes were like black marbles that sparkled with intrigue. The old priest who presided over the wedding had the features of a goat with his pointy ears, goatee and upturned eyebrows. Angel was told there were no other men around because they were out sheepherding.

The musicians were also women from the village. They played guitars, accordions and violins. Angel recognized the music since the pieces they played were also played in his village. The couple danced up a storm to "*El Valse de los Paños*" ("The Dance of the Handkerchiefs") and "*La Raspa*" ("The Rasp"). The women of the village joined in on the dancing.

During the New Mexico traditional wedding dance, called "*Entriega de los Novios*" ("The Delivery of the Newlyweds"), everyone in the village danced like a snake through the winding streets. Then the women took up the edges of their black shawls, lifted their arms like black wings and formed two lines, creating a path. Angel and Dulubina led the dancers through the long narrow passage. When they reached the end, they danced as a couple as the others formed a circle around them clapping and cheering.

The meal was beans, *chile*, squash, *verdolagas* (purslane) and tasty fried blood pudding. The wedding cake was made with the darkest chocolate Angel had ever seen. It was so delicious that it melted in his mouth. Dark, blood-red sparkling wine finished off the feast. The young couple had to spend their wedding night in the torreon, but Angel didn't mind.

Early the next morning, he woke up and found Dulubina and Doña Calada packed up and ready to leave. "Are we going somewhere?" he asked.

"To your village," Dulubina answered.

"You would never like it there," he argued.

Annoyed, Dulubina answered, "I want to experience new things and see the world outside these walls, and my mother must come with us."

Angel pleaded, "But we are happy here!"

Angry, Dulubina yelled, "Are you ashamed of me? Don't you love me?"

Angel realized this was important to Dulubina, and he could not disappoint her. He wondered how he would get Dulubina's dowry to his village. It consisted of sweet-smelling powders for her to put in the water when she bathed, a couple of strange black, leather-bound books and a methodically carved pine headboard with curious designs, letters and numbers. Angel wanted to leave the headboard, but Dulubina insisted, saying it was a precious family heirloom and she couldn't imagine leaving it behind. On second thought, Angel realized he had grown quite fond of the intricately carved smiling cherubs, hearts and beautiful dove with outspread wings. He prepared himself to pull the heavy load, but magically it moved with ease. They left on their journey.

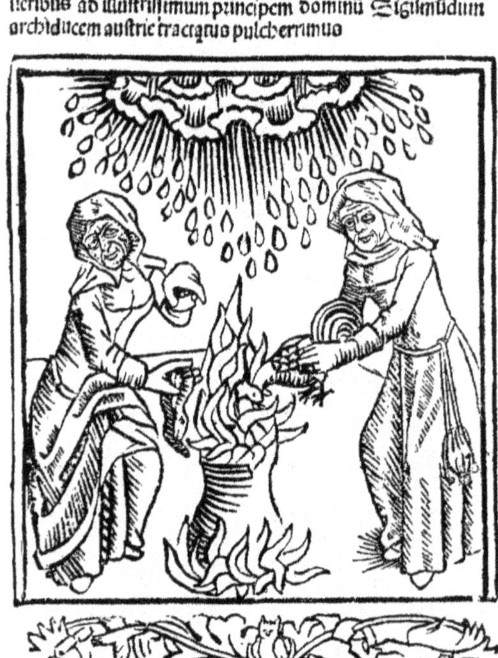


Witches brewing up a hailstorm, from the title page of Ulrich Molitor's *De Lanijs et Phitonicis Mulieribus*, printed by Cornelius de Zierikzee, Cologne, 1489. *Author's collection.*

As they entered the village, people stopped to stare; some whispered, and others looked shocked, but no one approached them. Angel wasn't surprised. They were probably jealous. He had dared to go where no one else had been and had returned alive and married to the most beautiful girl in the world.

Weeks passed, and Angel, for some strange reason, began to lose his appetite. He wasn't happy anymore, and he didn't feel well when he was awake. He began hiding some of his food because he knew Dulubina would insist he eat it. He also didn't want to hurt Doña Calada's feelings. She helped with the cooking, sewing and cleaning. Angel began to notice something very strange. As he slept less, he noticed his wife was mysteriously missing from the bed every night. The strong odor of sulfur began to wake him even from his deepest sleep. At first, Angel didn't give it much thought, but when it happened night after night, he became suspicious. "Was she meeting another man?" he wondered. He also noticed that the less he ate, the less he slept. One day, he decided not to eat at all. Angel pretended to be asleep that night. At the stroke of midnight, Dulubina got up from the bed. Angel waited for an eternal second and then followed her. He saw Dulubina join her mother outside the house. Angel could not believe what he was seeing. His beautiful wife and Doña Calada turned ugly. They swiftly transformed into owls and flew into the moonlit sky. He now knew the shocking truth. His wife and mother-in-law were witches.

Angel went back into the house, lit a lantern and was completely stunned when he saw the headboard. Instead of cherubs, he saw skulls. The hearts were now cauldrons. The number nine had changed to sixes, and the dove was an evil owl. Angel was scared out of his wits. He didn't know what to do. After thinking, he came up with a plan. He disconnected the headboard and carried it out of the house. It was so heavy that he had to drag it. He then got the two black leather books written in a language he couldn't understand and threw them on top of the headboard. He also got his wife's multicolored powders and sprinkled them over everything. In his shed, he found a container of kerosene. After pouring it over the wicked things, he lit them with a match. As they burned in the ominous night sky, he thought he could hear threatening movements in the trees, so he quickly ran into his house and bolted the door shut.

Needless to say, Angel went through a sleepless night praying and wondering where his wife and mother-in-law had gone and what evil things they might be up to. His imagination ran away with him. In the morning, he was afraid to go out of the house, but he finally got up the courage to check the ashes. To his amazement, nothing was there—not one ash, not one cinder. The headboard and everything had evaporated into thin air. Angel didn't know what to think. At the end of the day, he heard something outside the house, and when he looked out the window, he saw two owls up on a tree limb staring down at him. He quickly covered the window with the curtain, and at times when he heard the hoot of the owls, it sounded like one of them was angrily calling his name. He was terrified. The piercing eyes of the owls glowed, sending out beams of light that filled the room.

Angel was afraid to sleep. He spent the night fashioning crosses with whatever he could find. He placed them over each doorway and every window throughout the house. Even during the day, he was afraid to step outside. The owls returned each night searching for a way to get in. He occasionally fell asleep during the day, only to be awakened by the hoot of the owls as nighttime approached. Angel would begin his nightly ritual of lighting up his house from one end to the other with blessed candles. Holding onto a small wooden cross, he would continuously walk into each room until daybreak praying as loudly as he could, "By the power of God Almighty, I command all evildoers to leave me forever and to be relegated into the everlasting lake of fire, that they may never again touch me!"

The townspeople soon began to talk about Angel and what had made him go crazy. Their children learned how he had followed the moonlit path through the narrow gulley and hidden slopes to Los Voladeros. Upon Angel's return from his misadventure, they watched him proudly walk into town between two ugly old witches. He didn't seem to mind. Angel had been charmed, and all he could see was the most beautiful woman in the world. By the time he knew better, it was too late. Angel had been warned, but he did not heed the warnings of the Old Ones. The people now had a face and a name for a victim who had been captivated and charmed by the forbidden village in the clouds.

## The Headless Horseman of Santa Fé

*El que desea mal a su vecino, el suyo viene en camino.*
What goes around, comes around.

Among those who returned to Santa Fé in 1692 from El Paso del Norte, where the Spanish had sought refuge from the great Indian uprising in 1680, was Juan Espinoza. He was a man in his early twenties who had dreams of marrying and raising a family. He had already set his sights on a beautiful young lady named

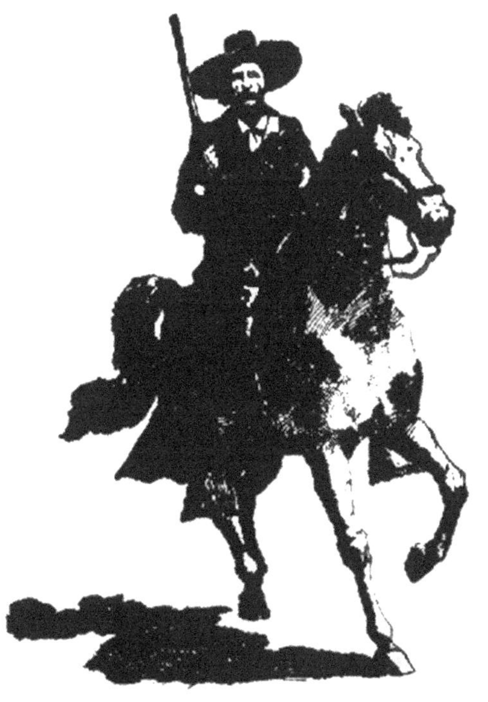

Santa Fé Spanish colonial presidio soldier, unknown artist. *Author's collection.*

Catalina Monroy, whom he had seen traveling with her family on the journey to Rio Arriba along the Camino Real. The arduous journey was made easier for Juan by glimpses of Catalina smiling and laughing with her sisters as the caravan trudged along. Catalina easily teased with those big dark eyes that sparkled like black sapphires in the sun. She often played with her long black hair and winked her eye as she cheerfully glanced at the boys on the trip. Juan Espinoza was quite taken by her, as were the others who vied for her attention.

Juan became a *soldado de cuera*—that is, a mounted soldier—who carried a multicolored leather shield and sported a lance used on campaigns against the Indians. He was stationed at the presidio in Santa Fé, and he saved every *real* he earned to buy land and build a house. In the meantime, Catalina had several suitors, and Juan had no idea that one of them was planning to ask her father for her hand in marriage. Juan's rival was none other than his best friend, Pedro Pino, who bunked next to him at the presidio and who would hear Juan singing Catalina's praises far into the night.

As luck would have it, Pedro was a tall, handsome, dashing young fellow with striking features and a magnetic personality. Poor Juan, in contrast, was short, stocky and had a ruddy complexion. He wasn't much fun to be with, but they say he was fiercely courageous in battle. Juan was not one to give up, and he was very determined in what he sought.

Now, the quaint Spanish proposal custom of the day in colonial New Mexico was for the suitor to take a highly respected and wise elder person to speak on his behalf when asking a father for his daughter's hand in marriage. The elder person could be a man or a woman and was more often than not a

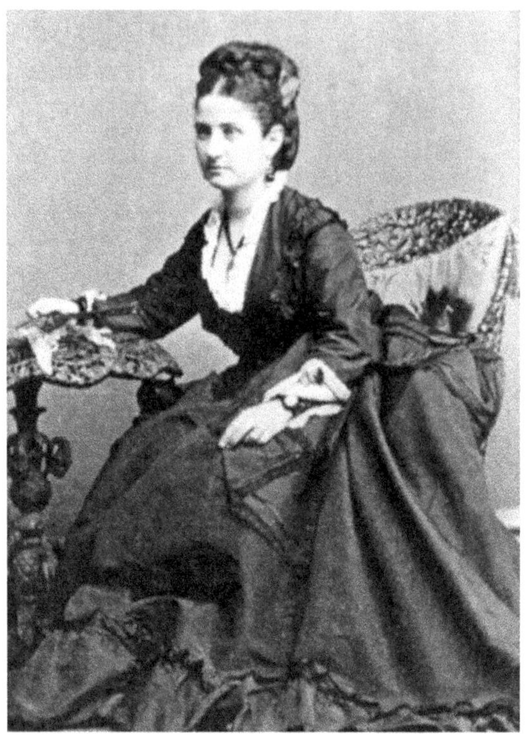

A typical woman of the Spanish colonial era and Mexican period of New Mexico, carte de visite photo, unknown photographer. *Author's collection.*

member of the family. Juan Espinoza's family had been killed during the Indian Revolt, and he had been taken as an orphan to El Paso del Norte to be raised. Juan thought very deeply about his problem and came up with a solution. He asked old Captain Alfredo Dominguez, who was a retired *presidio* officer, to help him. Captain Alfredo was more than honored to do it since Catalina's father, Don Vicente Monroy, was a close friend of his, and he also felt that Juan was a good man.

Lo and behold, when Don Alfredo and Juan went to Don Vicente's house and the captain presented the proposal on Juan's behalf, Catalina had already fallen in love with Pedro Pino. Juan's dreams were shattered when Catalina was called in to the *sala*, and she gave him *calabazas* when she was asked for her decision. If a young woman said, "*Calabazas*," which means pumpkins, that meant she was rejecting the proposal. Needless to say, Juan Espinoza was not pleased about this annoying turn of events. What was he to do? Juan spent many a sleepless night watching Pedro sleeping peacefully on his bunk. Pedro went often on campaigns on the Llano Estacado, the Staked Plains, where marauding Indians launched their attacks. But now, Juan's respect for Pedro had turned to hatred, and all he hoped for was that Pedro would be killed on one of the military campaigns.

One day, Juan heard some of his *compadres* talking about a pair of witches who lived in the Barrio de Analco in the oldest house in Santa Fé near the river. He overheard one of them saying that his luck had changed completely when he sought the advice of old Doña Filomena and her sister, Doña

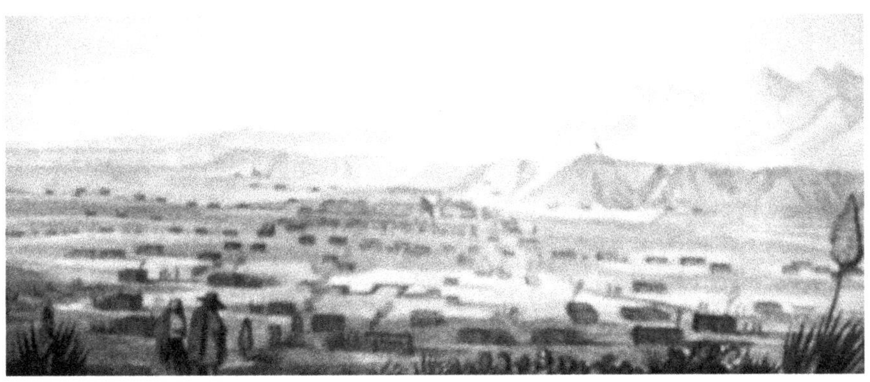

*Old Santa Fé.* From *Notes of a Military Reconnaissance, Fort Leavenworth, in Missouri, San Diego, in California, including part of the Arkansas, Del Norte, and Gila Rivers* by Lieutenant Colonel W.H. Emory (Washington, D.C., 1848). *Courtesy of the author.*

Lugarda. They had cast a spell for him that was making him rich. No one knows for sure whether or not the two old ladies were really witches, but one thing for certain is that they had strange powers, and they read from a black book they kept hidden in a hole in one of the rooms of their ancient house. It was claimed that with this book they could do just about anything, even transform themselves into owls or *bolas de lumbre*, balls of fire that danced in the moonlight. But those were just stories. Anyway, Juan thought he had found his answer.

Early the next day, Juan Espinoza went to see the old witches of Analco. He walked at a very rapid pace. He found them tending their fragrant herbs in a field near their house. They were dressed in black with long shawls, and they both had very crooked canes.

"Can you help me?" he asked them nervously.

"What is it that you want, Juan?" one of them answered.

As you can well imagine, Juan was stunned when he heard one of the old witches call him by his name. "How is it that you know who I am?" he asked.

"Oh, I can spot a Juan from a mile away. Juans have many, many powers. They can cure *mal ojo*, evil eye, with their spit; they can heal illnesses with their touch, or sometimes feel and see things that are not visible to others. Yes, you are a Juan. It's as plain as that eagle nose on your round face. So, Juan, what is it that you need?"

Juan explained his troubles to the old witches. They took him into the house, where they set about smelling and mixing herbs in a big black pot that hung over a fire in a corner fireplace. Juan wondered what the witches were up to while taking a pinch of this and a pinch of that, chanting and mixing it in the pot. After a while, there was a dead silence in the room as the witches meditated over the pot. Doña Filomena, who was older than Doña Lugarda, broke the silence. "There are two very important things that you must do, and you must follow this to the letter."

"What are they?" Juan asked.

"First, you must kill a pig. A piglet will do. Cut it open and eat its heart."

"May I cook it first?" Juan questioned meekly. "I love *matanzas*, *chicharones*, *carne adovada*, anything with pork in it, especially *chile colorado* (red chili). But the thought of a bloody raw heart? I don't think so."

"No, no, no!" responded the two witches at the same time. "We thought you would do whatever it would take for the girl of your dreams…but if this is not the case, you are wasting our time, and you must leave here at once!"

"No!" Juan cried. "I will do as you say."

"Very well," Lugarda said. "Then you will need to take this tea that we will give you to the girl's house and offer it as a gift to the girl and her father. After she drinks it, she will not be able to resist you. By the way, it will not have any effect on anyone other than the girl since it is a love potion that is meant only to work on her."

The witches strained and poured the precious liquid into a very pretty ruby red bottle and gently handed it to Juan. They charged him ten gold *escudos* for their hard work. This was a lot of money in those days. Juan nervously thanked the old witches, who danced around fondling the gold coins in their bony hands. The lovesick young man dashed out of the house with his liquid treasure and ran down the dusty road, wildly kicking up the dirt with his boots as he increased his speed. As he hurried home, he began to think. "I don't have time to kill a pig, and there is no way I can eat its heart. Besides, I have no time to waste. I have to get this potion to Catalina before it is too late. I will try to kill the pig later if the potion doesn't seem to work."

Juan Espinoza was soon at Don Vicente's house banging at the door. Don Vicente was quite upset with the loud noise. When he opened the door, he saw Juan holding a bottle with both hands and looking down at the ground. "I respectfully brought you and your very beautiful daughter a gift of tea," Juan said nervously. "I hope you both like it."

"Well, come in, then," Don Vicente said.

Don Vicente called for Catalina, and all three of them sat in the *cuarto de recibo*, which is a room where Hispanos in New Mexico receive their special guests. I must say that Juan felt very special, indeed. Don Vicente served the tea in three gorgeous but dainty blue and white cups from a set that had been brought to New Mexico all the way from China. "This is wonderful tea," Don Vicente said to Juan. "What kind of tea is this? Where did you get it?"

Juan, of course, lied. "I went to the Parada del Rancho de Las Golondrinas, where a caravan of goods had just arrived. It's imported from a faraway land that was recently discovered."

"*Bueno, esta muy delicioso*," Don Vicente said with a wide smile on his face. All three prayed to the *santos* to protect them as they drank the delicious tea. Just then, Juan noticed Catalina winking and smiling at him. His heart pounded like the hooves of a horse as they hit the ground, and he could hardly catch his breath. Juan was hoping Don Vicente hadn't noticed. He had beads of perspiration running down his face as he thought that the love potion was working on Catalina.

She suddenly got up and excused herself. She was feeling faint. Catalina, in a melodious voice, said, "Juan, please excuse me. I hope you will come and visit us again. We enjoyed your company. Thank you for your thoughtful gift."

Catalina's words kept swimming through Juan's head as he walked lovesick back to the *presidio*. During the following days, Juan couldn't really concentrate on his soldierly duties. Visions of the beautiful Catalina constantly filled his mind, even to the point that he could not eat or sleep. He couldn't help but give Pedro a sly smile every time he saw him. As a final act of poetic justice, Juan thought of asking his friend to be his best man at his and Catalina's wedding. Oh, what a grand thought he had! Juan would finally put Pedro in his place by winning what they both most desired. But then, something completely unexpected happened. Pedro excitedly walked up toward Juan one late afternoon, saying, "You'll never believe this, Juan. Catalina has consented to marrying me. She didn't give me *calabazas*! We're going to have a great big *fandango* with violin and guitar players, a huge *fiesta* where everyone is invited. What do you think of that, my friend?"

Juan's mouth fell wide open. It was opened up so wide that you could have driven a fully loaded *carreta* pulled by oxen in there and still have plenty of room left over. And his eyes were as big as saucers that spun around in circles. Oh, he was a sight to behold! Finally, a word roared out of Juan's mouth: "What?"

Without waiting for an answer, Juan ran to his horse, jumped on its back without a saddle and galloped off toward the witches' house. Juan was certain the witches had played a trick on him. Pedro stood there stunned and bewildered as Juan rode off.

After what seemed like an eternity, Juan Espinoza finally arrived at the witches' house. They were having a good old time baking bread in the *horno*

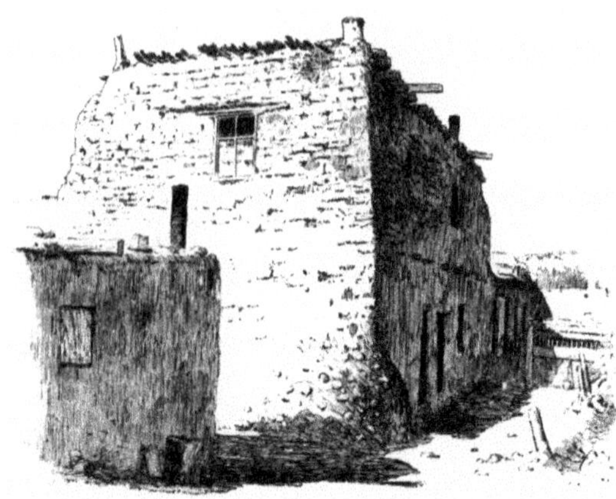

*The Oldest House in Santa Fe*, by F.M. Endlich. From *Harper's Weekly*, supplement, September 7, 1889. *Courtesy of the author.*

and stringing red *chile* pods for *ristras*. When Juan reined in his horse in front of them, they were totally perplexed. Jumping off his horse, he yelled, "You old witches lied! You said the love potion would work. It didn't! It didn't!"

Not batting an eye, Doña Filomena asked, "Did you follow all the steps? Did you do as you were told?"

"Yes I did! I did everything," Juan lied. "I want my gold coins back. You said it would work. That it was guaranteed."

Doña Filomena, quite perturbed, answered, "No, no, we cannot give you your money back. You did not follow our instructions. There is no blame on our part. It has never failed in the past. A deal is a deal!"

Just then, Juan drew his sword and began swinging it wildly above his head, yelling, "I'll kill you! I'll kill you old hags!"

It was quite a sight to see: the old witches running around with Juan chasing them. They didn't even think about the canes they definitely needed because of old age. As one witch went this way and the other went that way, one of them fell. Juan dashed right over to strike her with his sword. As he did so, he didn't notice a pointy rock on the ground that caught the tip of his boot. He fell with a thud, and his sword flipped out of his hand. One of the witches—and they don't say which one—quickly ran over, grabbed the sword, swung it around near Juan and cut off his head as he was pushing himself up from the ground. His bloody head went rolling down the road with its mouth and eyes wide open. Then, the strangest thing happened. Juan's body climbed up on the horse and went galloping off after the head, trying to scoop it up.

They say if you're out late at night on de Vargas Street near the old witches' house they now call "The Oldest House in the USA," there suddenly appears the shadow of an oval object rolling down the street. It may very well be the head of Juan Espinoza. In the old days, people from Santa Fé claimed that on certain nights, when the moon is bright, the sky is black and the sounds of Santa Fé have died down, you can hear the hooves of a galloping horse pounding against the road below. And if you dare to search the landscape, you just might catch a glimpse of the headless horseman chasing after his head.

## Fearless John/Juan Sin Miedo

*De la muerte y la suerte no hay nadie quien se escape.*
Death and luck do not discriminate.

It was said that Juan Valdez was not afraid of anything. He was the bravest man in the village of La Loma or anywhere else, for that matter. Once, he singlehandedly turned back a herd of stampeding buffaloes that threatened the lives of his *compadres* out on the plains. Juan was a *cibolero*, a buffalo hunter who never failed in bringing down the leader of the herd. He was also a Penitente who carried the heaviest cross and endured the hardest lashes. Everyone admired him. Juan Sin Miedo, they said, even laughed at Death herself.

Juan had many friends who often gathered at Don Vicente's store in Anton Chico to hear him talk about his exploits and how strong and brave he was. He had come close to death so many times and escaped. The townspeople often said, "Juan you have as many lives as a cat…not even death can catch you!" Juan began to believe what they said. It went to his head. At first, it was great fun to listen to Juan, but then his personality began to change. He dared others to stand up to him in any competition. Juan went as far as to laugh at Doña Aguida, who was known as the *bruja* who lived near the *arroyo* (creek). No one dared to bother her, and everyone left her to her own magic. After all, she didn't bother anyone. "I'm not afraid of your spells, you old hag!" Juan taunted the poor woman as she walked by one day.

Doña Aguida gave the bully a long, cold stare and continued on her way, hobbling along with her cane. "If you really knew magic, you'd straighten those crooked old legs of yours," Juan taunted, "and belief in witches is nothing but simple-minded superstition. I'll even wager that Doña Sebastiana riding in her Death Cart would be powerless against a good sharp axe." Mouths fell open and eyes widened when the others heard his desecrating

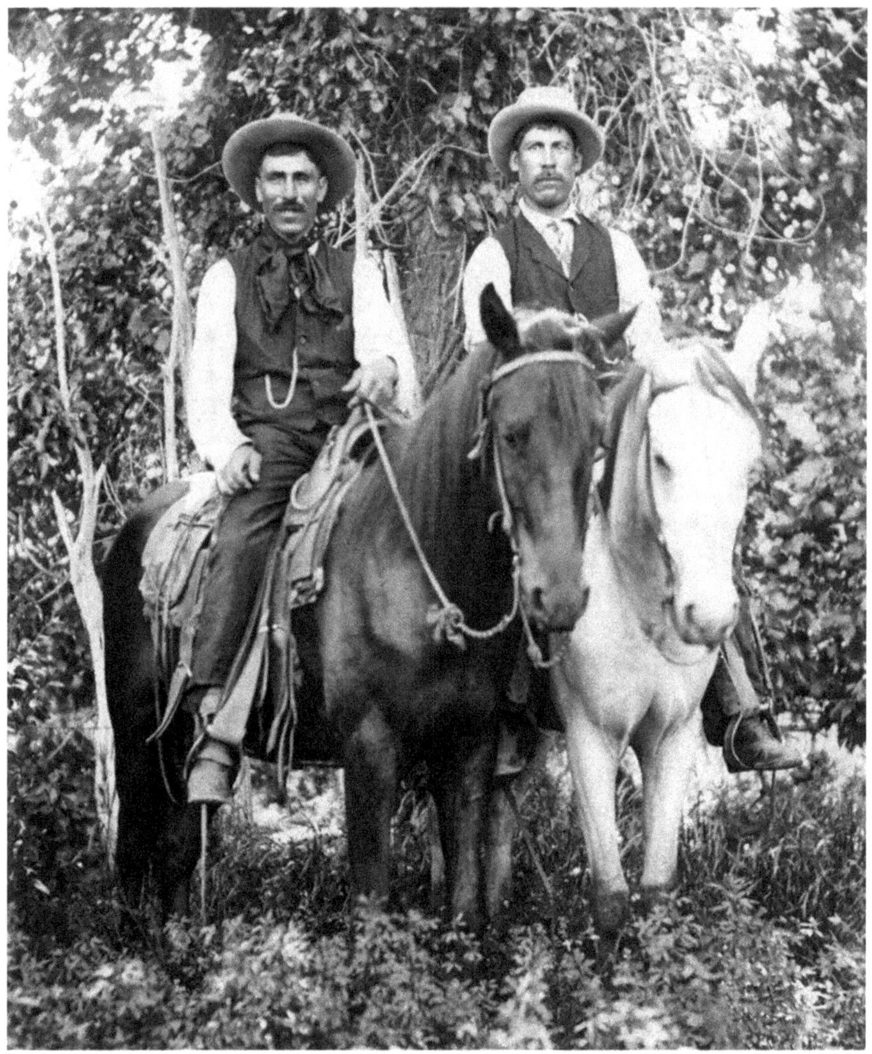

Ciboleros, buffalo hunters, unknown photographer, circa 1885. *Author's collection.*

words against the Angel of Death. Laughing at witches was a frightening thought, but to ridicule death in any way was unheard of.

Soon, Juan found fewer men paying attention at Don Vicente's when he would arrive there at noon each day. Juan's behavior was not that of a man to be respected and admired. He had lost favor with his fellow brothers at the *morada*, their meetinghouse, and friends and relatives avoided him like the plague. But Juan continued with his new ways. He didn't even realize that he was telling the stories to himself most of the time. It seemed as

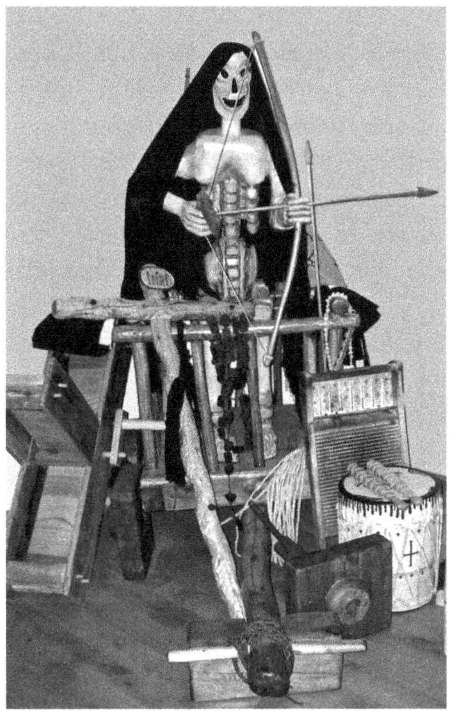

*Doña Sebastiana, New Mexico penitente death cart,* acrylic and gesso on pine. *©2000 Ray John de Aragón.*

though he loved the sound of his voice, and it didn't matter what anyone else thought.

One evening, Fearless John sat bored at home eating a late supper of *frijoles, chile* and *tortillas* and talking to himself. His stories were old. There was never anyone around to save with his bravery any more. He began to miss the sound of others talking and laughing and sharing their side of his tales. Now he felt quite alone for the very first time. What was he to do? Suddenly, he got a thought. Juan remembered that his Penitente brothers often had secret meetings at the morada. But why hadn't they called on him for such a long time? It must have been an oversight, he thought. He wondered if they might be there that night. It wouldn't hurt to check it out. He didn't have anything better to do. Juan slipped a pistol into his trousers in case he should meet up with a wild animal. He was always prepared for the worst. One could not be too careful, and that was the trick to his success at beating death.

The night was especially dark and gloomy. It was certainly not the kind of night one would venture out alone. But this bleakest, most uninviting night could not keep Juan Sin Miedo home. Soon, he reached the morada and was disappointed at not finding anyone there. Looking around with searching eyes, he saw three figures gathered near the old morada, which was no longer used except for an occasional wake. "Who died?" he wondered. Everyone knew everyone, and there were no secrets in a small village. Of course, it had been quite awhile since anyone had made conversation with him.

As Juan carefully approached the figures, he saw three men. "I'm Juan Sin Miedo," he said bluntly. "Who are you?" There was no answer. They definitely were strangers and probably up to no good. He pulled out his pistol and threatened to fire unless they answered his questions. Still, no one answered. Losing his temper, Juan fired his pistol into the air and demanded a response to his question. All three began to walk toward him in a menacing way. They had stern blank faces. "Stop or I'll shoot, and this time I won't miss!" Juan yelled. He fired his gun toward the men, aiming at their legs to stop them from coming closer. No one ever said he was stupid. There were three of them and only one of him. He had fought against many men at one time before, but these men were double his size, and he feared them for some odd reason. The shots didn't faze them. He was a good shot and couldn't understand how he kept missing them. They continued to walk toward him at a steady pace, with their arms and hands ready to attack. He thought of turning around and running away from the men as fast as he could. But he couldn't do it. What would people say? Juan had never backed down from a fight, and he wasn't going to start now. He stood his ground and prepared to fight. Juan threw the first blow. No sooner would he knock one man down than another was at his throat. They didn't seem to tire no matter how hard he fought. Finally, he was knocked out senseless.

This is the way his fellow Penitentes found him at daybreak the following day. Poor Juan was lying on the dirt, bloody and bruised. He recounted his story to the curious men who helped him up and took him into the old morada to wash and dress his wounds. Juan was not bragging but telling a story just like the good old days. This time, though, there was fear in his eyes. He wasn't the super human he had thought he was.

In the morada, Juan noticed corpses on tables at the far end of the room being prepared for a wake. "Who are the dead?" he asked.

"Oh, just a few ruffians killed the day before yesterday when they had a run in with the law. The bodies were brought in yesterday morning by wagon to see if we could do something for them. We felt a public wake and service would help their souls," one of the Penitentes responded.

"They're dressed just like the men who did this to me. Did they have friends who got away?" Juan asked.

"No," replied one of the villagers.

Fearless, John moved nearer to the dead men. He yelled in disbelief, "This man was the first to grab me by the throat!"

"Juan, that's impossible. Let us take you home. You'll feel better with some rest," the Penitentes replied.

"I shot at their legs," Juan continued. He lifted the pants near the bare feet of one of the dead men to check for a bullet wound. Wildly, he examined the second one and then the third. All three men had bullet wounds from the knees down.

"I can't believe it!" a brother exclaimed. "They didn't have those yesterday when we washed the bodies!"

Juan moved toward the open door of the morada and then stopped. Right outside was Doña Aguida. Her eyes glared into his. She held four poorly shaped dolls. With a smile, she dropped one. Juan yelled, "It's you!"

At that same moment, one of the dead bodies dropped from the table toward Doña Sebastiana sitting in her cart with her arrow and bow drawn. The arrow left the bow within seconds. Juan turned to see what had fallen. It was too late. Juan stood in disbelief as the arrow pierced his heart.

The Penitentes, who had been trying to lift the dead body, quickly rushed toward Juan, but he was dead. One of the Penitentes looked outside to see whom Juan had seen, but there was no one there. On the ground were four dolls and a large owl nearby glaring contentedly as it sat on a fence post.

And so the months passed by, and the strange sad story about Juan Sin Miedo and his bout with death and defeat was told and retold. Doña Sebastiana won the battle with the man who had cheated her so many times before. The Lenten season began, and the Penitentes gathered in the church to sing their *alabados* (hymns). Between hymns, they heard the sounds of someone whipping himself and moaning in the darkness of the choir loft. They finally got the nerve to look up. They say it was the spirit of Juan flagellating himself with a *disciplina* in eternal atonement for the wrongs he did in life. The Hermanos often hear his spirit in the old morada whipping his back during their rituals as they walk by late at night with their lanterns and *matracas* (rattles) during Lent. It reminds them not to challenge death, and it also reminds them to respectfully step aside when Doña Aguida wishes to walk by.

## Crisscrossed Witches

*Bruja roncando sale rodando.*
The witch who snoozes loses.

Felicitas and Gasparita knew about witches who lived in a very old *adobe* house about half a mile from their home. They were told never to go near there by day and especially not by night. It was said that late at night on very dark nights, the witches who lived there would change themselves into flaming balls of fire. As fireballs, they would dance around, having great fun in the nearby hills of La Ladera. The bright orange flames would go up and down and move all around just above the ground. Then the fireballs would disappear as mysteriously as they had appeared.

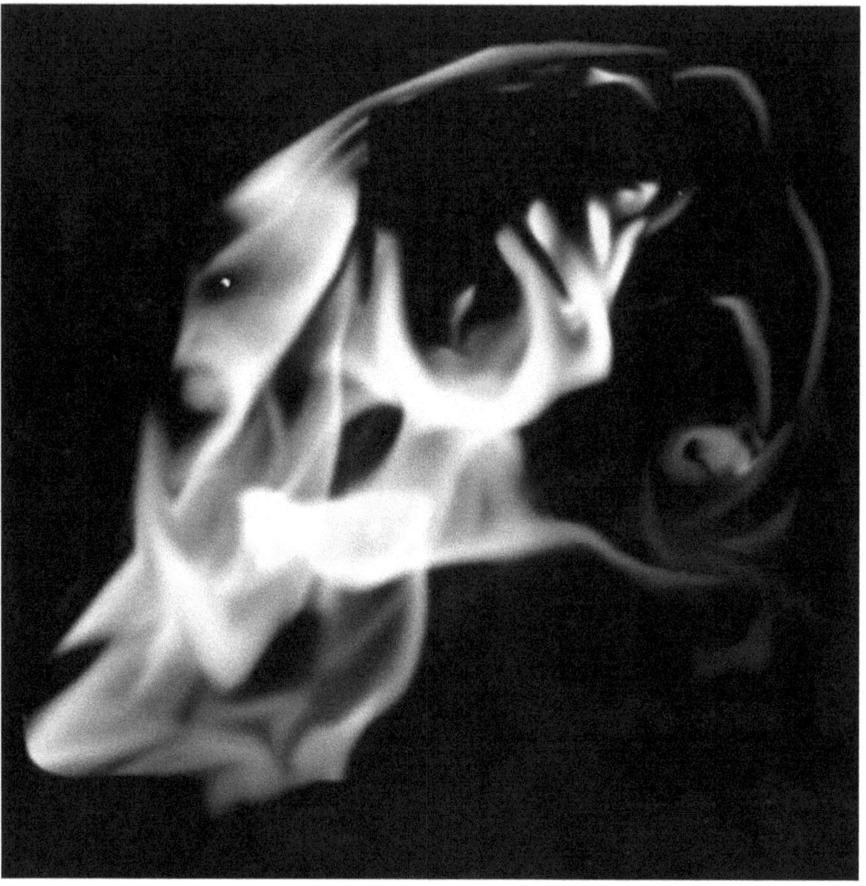

"Bolas de Lumbre," photograph, Lucia Dolores de Aragón. *Author's collection.*

One night, Felicitas and Gasparita were feeling very courageous, so they decided to hide in the bushes near the witches' house. Eventually, two old witches arrived, flying in on their brooms. One was tall, and the other was short. They walked into their home and closed the door behind them. In those days, doors were never locked. The two girls quietly tiptoed to the window. They watched as the two old witches carefully put their brooms to the right side of each of their beds, leaning them against the wall. Then they sat at the edge of their beds and sang a chant. Magically, their black-laced pointy shoes slipped off their feet and set down gently on the floor in front of their beds. The witches then rose up into the air and lay down flat on their backs on their beds. Soon, they were snoring away.

Felicitas and Gasparita waited for a while and then quickly followed through with a plan. They tiptoed into the house. Felicitas went for one of the brooms while Gasparita got the other. They quickly switched the brooms by putting the long broom of the tall witch by the short witch's bed and vice versa. Then, very carefully and very quietly, they switched the shoes, placing the right shoe on the left, and the left shoe on the right. Then they quietly walked out the door. Once outside, they walked over to the window and tapped loudly on the windowpane. The witches woke up and wildly looked around, rose up off their beds and reached for their brooms as they jumped into their magic shoes. They were totally confused by what was happening. Their legs suddenly crisscrossed. The right leg went to the left and the left leg went to the right. The tall witch was much too big for the small broom, while the short witch jumped on the tall witch's broom and it went out of control, running into and hitting everything in sight. The short witch screamed her head off. The witches soon became dizzy, and they crashed to the floor. They struggled to catch their feet to remove their shoes. No matter how hard they tried, their crooked old legs were all mixed up. They were completely helpless.

Felicitas and Gasparita ran and laughed all the way home. They had foiled the old witches with a simple trick.

II

# HISTORICAL OVERVIEW

## *Culture and Tradition*

New Mexico, as a land of mystery, miracles and enchantment, is vastly rich beyond the fabled Cities of Gold. The founding in 1610 of La Villa Real de la Santa Fé de San Francisco de Asís, the capital city of New Mexico, by the Oñate colonists further added to the significance and vast importance of El Camino Real. The Spanish divided the territory into two parts. La Bajada Hill near Santa Fé was the dividing line. The area north of the hill was called Rio Arriba (Upper River), and the area south of the hill was known as Rio Abajo (Lower River).

Many legends revolving around witches and ghosts that came from this period of New Mexico history have endured for centuries in various communities. For example, from Rio Arriba in the village of Bernal near Las Vegas, New Mexico, they tell a special story about Starvation Peak, which is located nearby. According to local lore, a mile or two from the peak, the Pecos Pueblo Indians attacked a group of Spanish colonists and soldiers during the Pueblo Indian Rebellion of 1680. While attempting to escape, the Spanish decided to climb the peak and take a stand at the top.

The Indians, numbering in the hundreds, soon had the base of the peak surrounded. Some of the warriors climbed up the peak, but they retreated after being met with a volley of rocks, bullets from the weapons of the Spanish soldiers, arrows that the women fired and anything else they could throw down at them, including burning fireballs they made with the brush. The onslaught continued for days, but the Spanish settlers and soldiers finally perished from thirst and starvation as they made their last stand at the top. Many years later, crosses were placed at the top of Starvation Peak to commemorate this memorable event. What is most interesting, however, is that area residents claim that on dark and silent nights they can hear faint unearthly cries coming from the peak. Although this story may have come from an actual historical event, tales are told at nearby villages of other strange occurrences.

Settlers in both the Rio Arriba and the Rio Abajo also had many stories and legends about the waterways that were unique to their settlements.

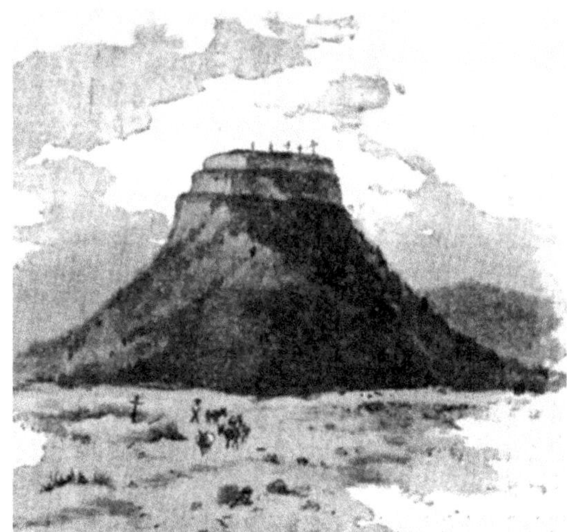

*Left*: *Starvation Peak*, by Charles Graham. From *Harper's Weekly* 35, no. 1806 (1891). *Author's collection.*

*Below*: "Alameda Acequia," photograph. *©2009 Ramon Juan Carlos de Aragón.*

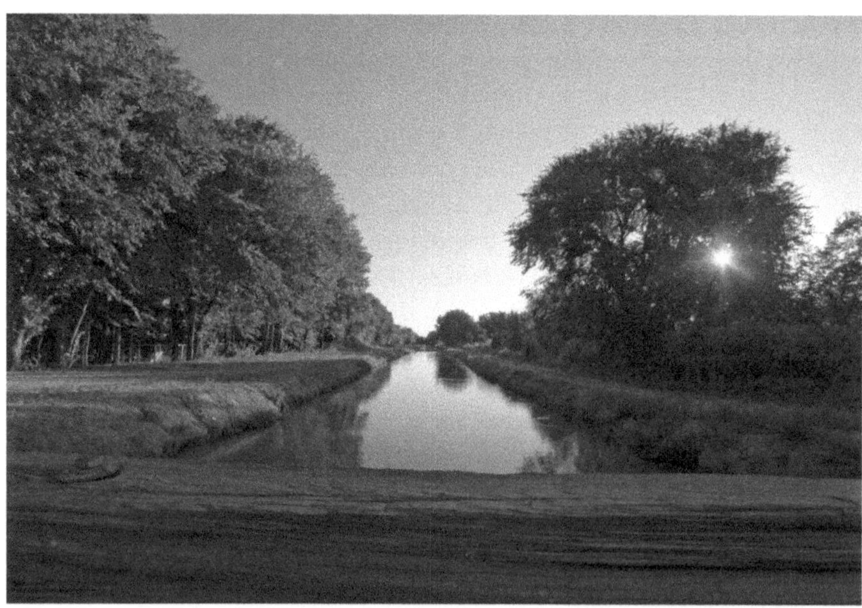

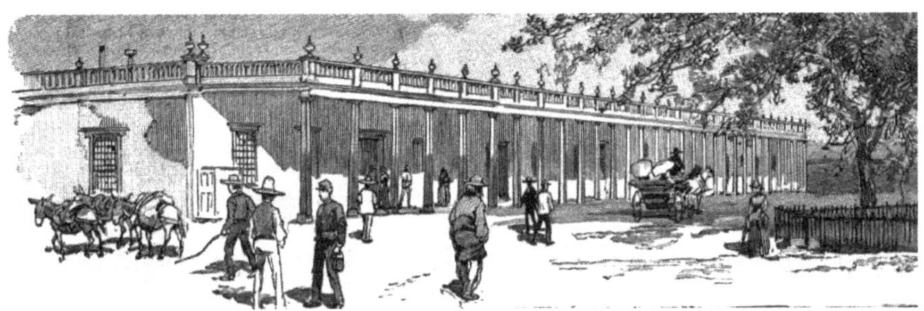

*The Governor's Palace*, in which Lew Wallace wrote *Ben-Hur*, drawn by Charles Graham. From *Harper's Weekly* 34, no. 1752 (July 19, 1890). *Courtesy of the author.*

To avert famine in New Mexico, the people put a tremendous amount of labor into the hand-dug gravity-flowing channels that sustained the Spanish colonial villages and churches. It is believed that the nearly one thousand *acequias* or ditches in New Mexico were the result of the hard work and efforts of the Franciscan friars and Spanish colonists. Tomé—a peaceful little village south of Albuquerque, New Mexico, that depended on these acequias for its survival—was also during this time an important center of trade and commerce on the Camino Real. From this area we get the stories like that of "Juan Goche" and "The Merry Ghost."

The city of Santa Fé was another major trade and exporting center that extended outward with the establishment of the Spanish Trail into California and the Santa Fé Trail into Missouri in the late eighteenth and early nineteenth centuries. New Mexico Hispanic merchants and traders traveled long distances on these roads to sell and trade goods such as weaving, tin and iron works, handmade furniture and religious images. During the Spanish colonial era, the White Sands near the Camino Real was an area where the skeletons of horses, oxen and sometimes protruding human skeletons and skulls could be found. Buzzards flying above and decaying bodies below could be seen. This provided a setting for folklore such as "The Legend of La Pavura Blanca."

Not unlike the rest of the world, New Mexico was also in an age of superstition, belief in witches and other unearthly beings. It was believed that some unexplained illnesses were the result of curses or other evil practices. *Curanderas* (medicine women) were sometimes called upon to cure *espanto* when the patient was severely frightened by what he or she saw. Anyone horror-stricken by a bad scare called *susto* also required special attention. Locally produced beeswax candles were always lit before sacred images to pray. If a candle burned blue, however, that meant that a ghost was present

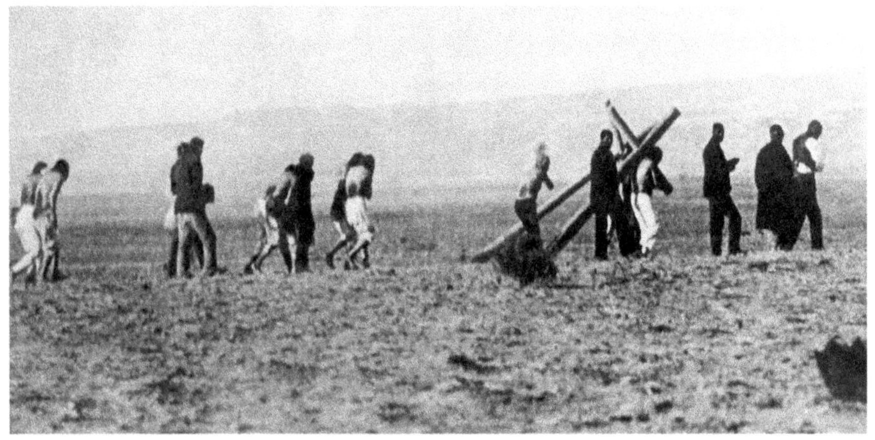

New Mexico Penitentes, photo by E.E. Wentworth Layton, 1905. *Author's collection.*

nearby. Therefore, *incienso*, or incense, had to be used for purification to stimulate the presence of good and to drive away evil. In the Rio Abajo, Antonio Menchero was a dreaded sorcerer. In Rio Arriba, Atole Caliente was a dreaded witch. The curanderas had to pray every day to receive special graces from God to help them against witches and sorcerers.

These traditions tell us a great deal about how people felt about life and death, their superstitions and religious beliefs. These are exemplified in the story of Don Bernardo Abeyta around the year 1810. Don Bernardo, an influential leader of the Penitente Brotherhood, was out during Holy Week on the night of Good Friday doing penance, including self-flagellation on the hills of El Potrero. As Don Bernardo sang his *alabados*, it is said he saw a bright light coming out of the ground on one of the hills near the Santa Cruz River. He went to see what it was and discovered that the mysterious light was coming from a wooden object that was sticking out of the ground. Don Bernardo scraped around the wood with his fingers. To his amazement, his treasure turned out to be a large crucifix with a greenish-tinged corpus of Christ.

Don Bernardo decided to leave the crucifix at the site, and the next morning he called on his neighbors to go see his precious find. Some of his fellow Penitentes traveled to the church at Santa Cruz to tell Fray Sebastian Alvarez about it. The fray picked it up out of the hole, and they all carried it to the church and placed it near the main altar after a ceremony composed of prayers and singing. The next morning, the crucifix was gone. Fray Sebastian and some of the parishioners came to the conclusion that it had been stolen, but sometime later, it was rediscovered at the original location. The crucifix was once again taken to the church, and it was hung on the wall, but just like before, it disappeared and was back in the hole near the river. After this happened the third time, it was felt that for some strange reason the crucifix had to stay where it was found.

In 1814, Don Bernardo Abeyta, along with other Penitentes, began the construction of a *santuario*, a sanctuary, which was to be a permanent church to hold the crucifix. Now internationally known as the Santuario de Chimayo, this shrine is one of the most popular pilgrimage sites in the world, which has resulted in numerous miraculous cures and for some an escape from death.

When the Spanish arrived in the New World, they brought their own death beliefs. Ancient epidemics that gave rise to mans' preoccupation with death because of mass suffering touched the lives of everyone. These death beliefs encouraged the Spanish explorer Ponce de Leon to search for miraculous water that could restore youth and vitality, which led to the discovery of Florida in 1513. Other explorers embraced the uniqueness of New Mexico's mountainous wonders, beautiful valleys and awesome splendor, which they call the "Land of Enchantment." To the religious Hispanic New Mexicans of the day, everything had a meaning and a purpose. They told stories to show us that one better be prepared with a clear heart and soul because you never know when your time will come and the spirits of the dead will rise and roam around to take the living along with them.

## The Merry Ghost

*Los Fantasmas se espantan con los vivos.*
You have to be more afraid of the living than the dead.

Not all ghosts are frightful and scary. There are some like the *fantasma alegre*, the merry ghost of La Ladera in the village of Tomé. Some say the ghost liked drinking wine.

Felicitas Vallejos Jaramillo was a beautiful widow with hair as black as the darkest night and brilliant blue eyes. Felicitas owned many acres of land in La Ladera. She had married at a very young age to a much older man. After the death of her husband, she supported her family by sewing wedding dresses and other clothing for the people in her village. One day, while Felicitas was visiting family in Adelino, also a little community within the village of Tomé, a handsome red-haired stranger with sky blue eyes rode into town on a beautiful white stallion. News traveled quickly that the stranger, Enrique Calles, was

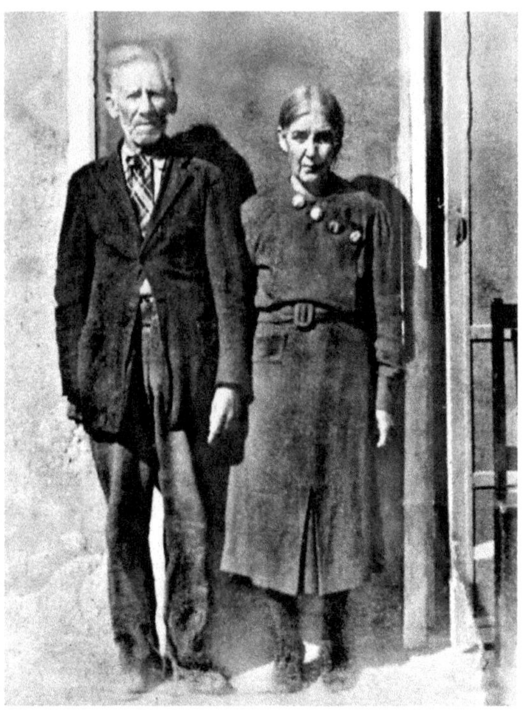

Enrique Calles (1858–1959) and Felicitas Vallejos Calles (1883–1976). Enrique, the sixth great-grandson of Captain Don Bernardo de Miera y Pacheco, soldier, mapmaker and later *santero*, served under Governor de Anza in several campaigns. He was also the fourth great-grandson of Don Manuel Calles, *santero*, and the Calleses were grandparents of Rosa María Calles. Photograph circa 1940s. *Courtesy Adolfo Calles.*

an heir to many acres of land in Adelino, and he had come to claim his land. Felicitas was crossing the dirt road to return home when Enrique rode up beside her and asked if she needed a ride home. "I have walked through here many times on my own and have managed just fine, Señor," she said curtly as she walked away.

"You are going to marry me someday," he said. Then he smiled and rode away.

Felicitas pretended not to hear, but she also smiled all the way home.

Enrique and Felicitas did marry. Eventually, Felicitas' children from her previous marriage wanted to start their own families, and they preferred building their homes in Adelino. They had jobs away from home and were doing well. The girls had also married, and their husbands had plenty of land of their own. Enrique traded his land in Adelino for their land in La Ladera. He felt there were too many people in Adelino. Enrique loved the open space in La Ladera for farming.

Enrique and Felicitas had many acres planted with white, purple and red grapevines. He made wine the old way by stomping and mashing the grapes. The happy couple had three sons, Elias, José and Adolfo. Elias rarely got into trouble, but José and Adolfo were always full of mischief. Felicitas spent a lot of time scolding them, but that didn't do much good since she laughed at their pranks. This only added more fuel to the fire. She saved them from many whippings by reminding Enrique about his wild escapades up until the time they had gotten married. The boys enjoyed wine making but not the chores that went along with it.

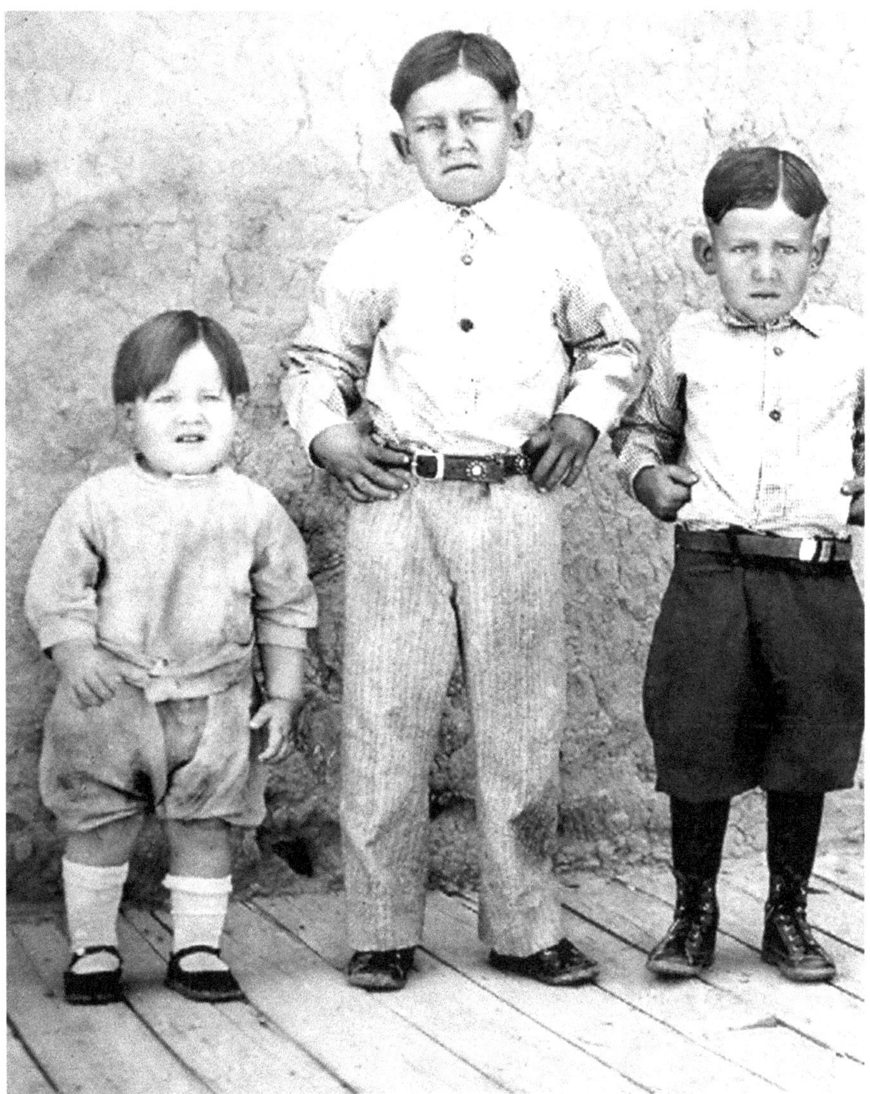

Adolfo, Elias and José Calles, photo, circa 1931. *Courtesy Rosa María Calles.*

Before the grapes were picked for making wine, there was much work to be done prior to the harvesting. Eventually, the grapes were ripe and ready for picking. Adolfo and José had to pick ripened grapes and put them in baskets. Grape picking took days because there were so many vines. Once all of the grapes were picked, the next step was to wash them with well water and put them into a huge oblong galvanized metal tub. Their mother would place a large cloth next to the tub, have the boys roll up their pants and then wash and scrub their feet so they could help mash the grapes. It was great fun for the two, who had to resist pushing each other and falling into the grape mash.

The next step was to scoop up the juice with a pitcher and pour it into a manta, a cotton cloth placed in a smaller tub. The cloth would be squeezed until every last precious drop of liquid came out of it. Enrique processed the juice by adding sugar, acid, nutrients and yeast. This mixture was carried into the large storage room that had a dirt floor and adobe walls, and it was poured into a large wooden barrel to be fermented. The wine processing took months and months, and it took the hands and the taste buds of an expert to make the different wines perfect.

These were hard times, and the people planted their gardens of green *chile*, *calabacitas*, tomatoes, corn, beans and all the vegetables they ate. Fields of alfalfa were planted to feed the livestock. They also raised pigs, cows, sheep and goats and had hundreds of turkeys. The women got together to make the *ristras* of red *chile*, can and dry fruits and vegetables, make jams and jelly and do everything else that needed to be done before the cold weather arrived.

Enrique and Felicitas worked very hard, and they expected the rest of the family to work hard also. Adolfo didn't mind most of the other work, but he hated taking care of the turkeys. It was hard keeping the turkeys from the garden and the grapes. He knew if the turkeys got into the crops, he would be punished. The turkeys were stubborn and fast. They kept him on his feet all day. When things were quiet and the turkeys were content after being fed, he would occasionally take a nap in the fields only to wake up and see that the turkeys had eaten some of the crops. He would pick up rocks and run around frantically toward the turkeys, scaring them out of the fields. Some would die in the process. Adolfo would be too scared to tell his parents, so he would dig holes in the ground and bury them. They had so many turkeys that they were never missed.

Everything was fine until his brother Elias caught him burying a dead turkey. Of course, he told his parents, and Adolfo got a whipping. As the boys got older, their chores increased, and so did the length of their days. They would get up early and do what they could before school and then were expected to finish the rest of the work in the evenings. Adolfo enjoyed school, and he was always proud of his good grades.

It was good to go to school, but in farming communities, the children only attended school during the fall and winter months. During the spring and summer, most Hispano families worked on their farms to prepare for the winter, and they herded cattle and held *rodeos* for entertainment and fun.

Adolfo and José attended school in Adelino. The principal, Ismael Sánchez, and the head teacher, Manuel Sánchez, were brothers. Manuel had a wooden leg, so it was hard for him to walk around and chase after the kids, but he did have a leather whip that he would crack when they were out of line.

It was a very beautiful sunny and warm winter day when Manuel Sánchez decided to take his students outside to play. Adolfo and José were running around the field chasing each other. Manuel felt like getting on the swing that was hanging from a cottonwood tree limb. After just sitting there for a few minutes, he decided to swing, so he called Adolfo, who was running by, to push him. Adolfo didn't want to do it, but he had to do what his teacher told him. The wooden-legged teacher warned him, "Don't push me too hard or too high!"

"I won't," the boy said obediently.

The swing was just a wooden board that was attached to a very high tree limb with two long, thick ropes.

At first, Adolfo only pushed him lightly, but then when he saw that his teacher wasn't saying anything as he started to push a little harder, he got bolder. It finally got to the point that he decided to go for one big, almighty push. Adolfo was getting bored. He used all the strength that his skinny body could muster and gave it his all. To the young boy's amazement, the ropes twisted and turned, and the poor wooden-legged teacher was headed straight for the tree. The teacher was screaming for help, but there was nothing poor Adolfo could do. He just stood there in disbelief as his teacher's one good leg and one wooden leg went up, slammed into the tree and got stuck. Then slowly, very slowly, his legs slid, and the teacher fell to the ground. The wooden leg had to be fixed. Needless to say, Adolfo was punished.

The punishment for Adolfo was to carry wood and coal from the shed for the wood stoves in the schoolhouse for two weeks. The teacher was surprised when José volunteered to help his brother. One day, the two boys got to the shed, and José pulled out two pouches of tobacco. One was Golden Grain, and the other one was Duke. José had his yellow sheets of paper, so they rolled their cigarettes, struck up some matches and puffed away. Then they hid the tobacco and papers for their next day's trip. After a few days, Sánchez started noticing that the boys were too eager to go out to the shed to get the wood and coal. Before they left, he told them, "Take your time, boys. It isn't cold today, so there's no need to hurry." This would give the crafty old teacher enough time to walk with his wooden leg to see what the two were up to. Adolfo and José didn't suspect a thing, so they went off whistling to the shed.

A few minutes later, Manuel Sánchez hobbled up quietly behind the building and heard some laughing. He moved very slowly toward the front and caught the two boys lighting up a second cigarette. The teacher took Adolfo and José to the principal. It was time, once again, to take out the leather strap. Of course, when they got home and their parents found out what had happened, they would be whipped once again.

It was finally spring, and school would soon be out. Manuel Sánchez decided the class would enjoy an outing to the Ojuelos. The Ojuelos was a favorite spot for picnics about fifteen miles east of school. It was an area with refreshing springs, a large pond to fish in, shade trees and little hills, valleys and *arroyos* to run and play. The great Indian fighter and Civil War hero Colonel Manuel Chávez, El Leoncito, had his *hacienda* at the Ojuelos back in the 1860s along with his wife, Vicenta. The teacher knew that Adolfo could easily get a flatbed wagon for the trip, and so he asked him if he would. Adolfo was anxious for some fun and mischief. He had forgotten all the whippings he had gotten during the winter.

Adolfo and José were able to borrow the flatbed wagon that they used to carry hay from their father. They asked their father if they could use his horse, Espantajo (Spook), to pull the wagon. Don Enrique reminded them that Espantajo was a great horse, but he had one little fault. If you let the reins hit his hind legs, the horse would take off in a mad dash. Other than that, Espantajo was perfectly all right. José asked to ride alongside the wagon on his own horse. Of course, Don Enrique knew Adolfo could control Espantajo, so he didn't see any problem with the arrangement.

Manuel Sánchez and the whole class were excited about the trip. The journey started off very nicely. The teacher and the students sat on the flatbed as Adolfo pulled lightly on the reins and José rode his horse alongside the wagon at a slow pace. The group went happily along singing songs. They were finally out in the llano on their way to the Ojuelos. José sped up on his horse, yelling back and daring Adolfo to catch up to him. Adolfo couldn't resist the dare. He took the reins and let them slap the hind legs of the horse. Espantajo jumped up and then took off. The teacher with the wooden leg yelled at the top of his voice as one of the students fell off the wagon and tumbled onto the ground. The rest of the students tried to find something to hold onto, but eventually all of them found themselves on the ground. Sánchez could not hold on any longer, either. He yelled, "Adolfito, you will pay for this!" as he broke his fall on a pile of large tumbleweeds. The teacher waved his fists threateningly in the air.

José returned on his horse to see what the result of their deed was. In the meantime, Adolfo had gotten Espantajo to calm down and reined him in to a stop. As the two watched from a distance, Don Manuel helped some of their classmates up off the ground. A few had tumbleweeds stuck to their clothes, and others were covered with dirt. One of the girls cried as the teacher pulled the tangled tumbleweeds and sticks from her hair. Some of the children jumped and laughed and wanted to do it all over again. "That was fun!" they yelled. This only aggravated the old teacher.

Manuel Sánchez rounded up his students, and they started their return to the school. Adolfo's home wasn't far away, and the teacher knew it would give him a chance to inform Don Enrique about what Adolfo and José had done. Adolfo and José had thought this would be fun to do, but as usual they had forgotten to consider the consequences. They talked and decided that they would try to convince the teacher it was all an accident. They reached the group, and Adolfo tried to speak to Don Manuel, but he wouldn't hear of it. The students laughed and told stories about their adventure and their tumble off the wagon for many years. That night, Adolfo and José had to listen to their mother, Felicitas, who warned them about paying dearly for bad deeds.

Felicitas told them the story about their uncle Proceso and her nephew Rudolfo, the son of her brother Adolfo. It seems that Proceso was always having a great time out on the town, and he was not a good influence on her nephew. Proceso was always drinking wine, laughing, joking and playing pranks for fun. That is the way he spent his entire life. He never took anything seriously and thought that everything was a joke. When he died, she said, he started appearing at night to pay for what he had done, and then she warned her sons, "He'll let us know what you're up to if you're fooling around again. *Allí veran lo que les va a pasar*—wait till you see what will happen to you."

Adolfo and José started to think that the story might possibly be true because they heard tales at school about the Fantasma Alegre, the Happy Ghost, who could be heard laughing and singing. It was claimed around Tomé, Adelino and La Ladera that a ghost would wander about late at night playing tricks on people and then would fade away giggling. No one knew when he would suddenly appear. The two boys wondered if the ghost could be that of their uncle Proceso, but they didn't let it bother them too much.

One day, Adolfo and José came up with a plan. They saw where their father's favorite large barrel of white wine was leaning up against the back wall of the *cochera*, a storage room where wine was allowed to ferment. They decided to dig a hole through the thick adobe wall from the outside to the barrel of wine. This took a few days of hard work, and they would cover up the hole with adobe bricks so that it couldn't be seen. After they finally got to the barrel, they drilled a hole into it and stuck in a thin rubber hose to siphon some of the wine out. During all of this hard work, Adolfo and José took turns being the lookout. Needless to say, they got more than a taste of wine.

Adolfo and José were teenagers, and they liked being popular with the girls. Their father had a favorite jet-black mare he called Sombra Negra, Black Shadow. They asked for permission to move out of the bedroom where they had slept in the house. Elias, their older brother, was more than happy to have his own room, and he encouraged their parents to let his brothers move into the *despensa*. The despensa was where their uncle Proceso had stayed when he was alive. It was a room attached to the cochera. José came up with a plan. He told Adolfo that they should sleep with their hats on at night and cover themselves up to their heads. This way, their parents would get used to seeing them in bed that way. He knew Don Enrique and Felicitas always checked up on them at night to make sure they were in their room asleep. In time, Adolfo and José started to sneak out of their room and meet with some friends. Of course, they were popular since they always took some of their father's favorite wine with them. They used sticks to hold their hats in place and sheep's wool to form the shapes of their bodies under the blankets. Their parents checked in on them as usual and marveled at how soundly they slept.

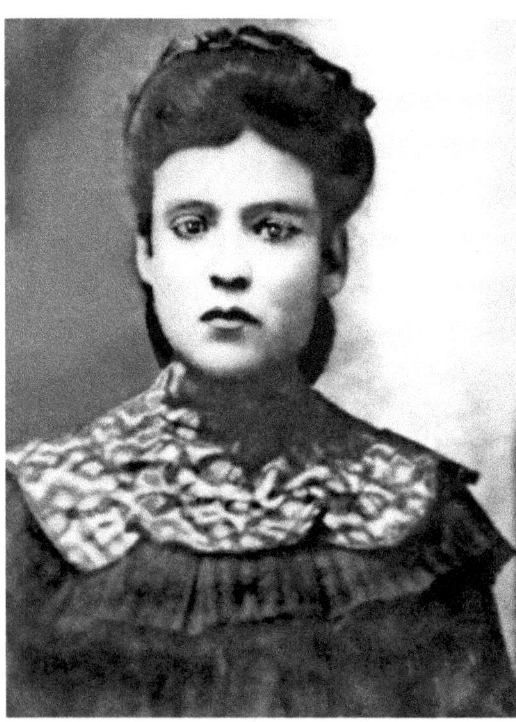

Felicitas Vallejos Calles, tinted photo, late nineteenth century. *Courtesy Rosa María Calles.*

The first thing Don Enrique did each morning was to go out to greet his horse, feed it and give it water. One day, he saw that his horse was warm and a little sweaty. He had also been wondering why his prized wine in the barrel had been going down. At breakfast, he told his wife about it, and she answered, "Maybe the ghost of Proceso is coming back to drink the wine and ride your horse." Adolfo and José just looked at each other.

One night, Enrique thought he heard a horse outside, so he went out to check on Sombra Negra. The horse was gone. He rushed into the boys' bedroom, picked up their hats and discovered that they were also gone. He came up with an idea that might scare the daylights out of them and teach them a real lesson. Don Enrique told Felicitas what the boys had done. He asked her for a white sheet, cut two holes in it and put it over his head. Felicitas didn't think it was a good idea, but he insisted. He told her to go to bed and that he would sleep in the despensa until the boys returned. He waited patiently for his sons to get home.

Finally, the disobedient sons got home and walked Sombra Negra and the other horse to their stalls. They had drunk a little too much wine. They laughed as they wondered if their parents really believed the ghost of Proceso was drinking the wine. Don Enrique waited for the boys to put the horses in their stalls. Adolfo and José walked quietly and slowly toward their room. As they neared the despensa, the door swung open, loudly hitting the side of the wall. The boys stopped in their tracks, scared to death. A white ghost came out, waving its arms up and down and making frightening sounds. Adolfo and José didn't know what to do. José yelled out, "No ghost is taking me!" He quickly picked up a rock and swung it at the ghost as hard as he could.

The ghost cried out, "*¡Ay Dios mío!*" (Oh my God!) and fell to the ground. Felicitas ran out of the house when she heard the screams.

"*Mamá*," the boys said, " we caught the ghost who's been drinking the wine!"

## Night Specter

*El que guarda el oro, el oro lo guarda.*
He who saves gold is kept by gold.

There's a beautiful little valley near Arroyo Hondo where the villagers tell a story about something very strange that happened many years ago. If anyone were to travel by this peaceful area by day, nothing unusual would catch their attention except that the entire window frames and doors of the houses are painted blue. This quaint old place used the color blue to keep evil away from its homes. Blue invoked the protection of the blue mantel of Mary, the mother of Christ. This was the tradition in New Mexico since Spanish colonial times.

Many, many years ago, there lived a family on a farm at the foot of one of the hills near Arroyo Hondo. The father was named Andres; the mother, Sinforosa; and their son, Felipe. Don Andres was much older than Doña Sinforosa. Andres was very stern in his ways and also very stingy with his riches. He had saved most of his money, but no one knew where he kept it. He didn't trust banks or anyone else with his money, not even his family. Doña Sinforosa had learned to keep very quiet and do all of the chores required by Don Andres without complaining. As the years passed, she became resentful. Don Andres had not allowed her to have any friends, and having a son who resembled Don Andres only added to her misery. She didn't show much affection for her unfortunate son Felipe. She couldn't even stand to look at him because he reminded her of her husband, whom she had grown to hate. Felipe often wondered why his parents didn't love him.

Doña Sinforosa was happy about one thing now that her son was growing older. Felipe could care for the farm animals and the crops while she took care of the household chores and cooked. Also, while Don Andres spent time outside watching his son work and yelling at him to do better or work faster, she had some peaceful moments alone in the house. She took time in the house to search for her husband's hidden treasure. Andres knew what his wife was up to, but he also knew that unless he told her where the treasure was, she would never find it.

Eventually, Sinforosa's husband grew so old that he could no longer move around. One day, Felipe returned home and found that his father had died. Don Andres had given his wife detailed instructions about the kind of burial and services he wanted. He warned her that if she did not place all of the money that was left after the expenses with him in the coffin, he would come back from the dead to haunt her. Sinforosa argued that she needed some of the money to survive after he was gone. But he wouldn't hear of it. He felt she was fortunate that he was leaving her his land and farm animals so that she could earn the money she needed to feed herself and Felipe. Andres made Sinforosa swear on the Bible that she would follow his wishes or he would never reveal where the money was hidden. She knew this was a serious thing because, in those days, to make a promise on the Bible and then to break it meant you had sold your soul to the devil. Sinforosa finally made the promise, and Andres told her where the money was as he breathed his last breath.

Of course, Sinforosa didn't do as she had promised. All that nonsense about the devil was pure superstition, she thought. What could Andres do to her now that he was dead? She did not even purchase a coffin. She was not

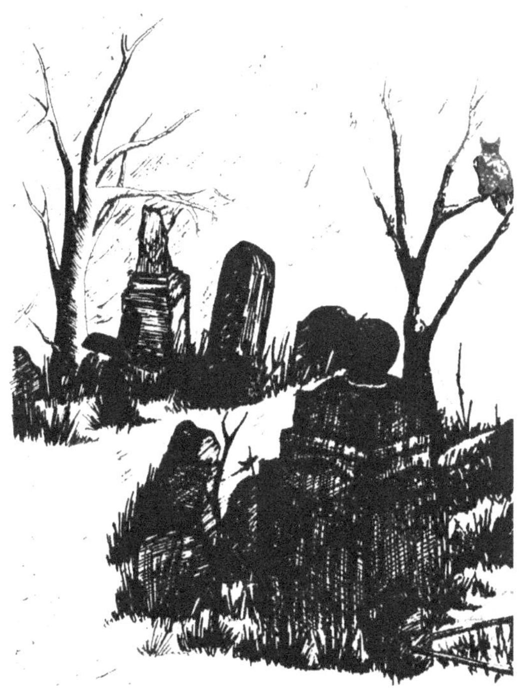

Pen-and-ink drawing. *©1980 Rosa María Calles.*

going to waste money on a funeral. The village priest offered his services, but she turned him away. Felipe dug the grave at the cemetery as his mother ordered. The villagers tried to offer condolences, but she ignored them. After all, they might expect something in return. Now that she owned all that her husband had saved through his many miserable years, she was not letting anyone have any of it, including her son.

Sinforosa would occasionally remember her husband's curse, but eventually she forgot all about it. Things did not improve for Felipe. Felipe worked just as hard as before. Every penny he made from the sale of the crops, Sinforosa added to the treasure of silver and gold coins that her husband had saved. As the years passed by, the old woman became very sick. Sinforosa had become suspicious of her son. She covered the kitchen windows with black cloth. The old woman always had her son leave when she took out some of her treasure because she was too afraid that he would take it and leave her to take care of herself. Even when it became too difficult to walk, she still followed him to the door and locked it once he was outside.

More years passed by, and the sick old woman could no longer do anything in the house. Felipe could not take care of the animals, the land, the house and his mother, too. Sinforosa needed her son by her side all the time, so she decided to sell all of the farm animals. Felipe sold them as he was told. On his way back home with the money, Felipe actually felt happy. He had never felt this way before. He had gotten much more money for the animals than he or his mother had expected. People were anxious to buy the animals he had cared for. They were well fed and very healthy. At least he felt he was good at something. He had never held so much money in his hands before. He thought, "Surely Mother will be so happy. She might even reward me with a little of the money since it was I who always cared for the animals." He soon learned this was not to be the case. Doña Sinforosa took the money from his hands and chased him away to do his chores in the garden. Instead of expressing gratitude, she wondered if he had cheated her out of any of the money.

More time passed, and now the old woman could scarcely move from the bed. Felipe spent most of his time taking care of his mother. Needless to say, the farm was running down. He rarely spoke and never complained. Sinforosa was quite feeble and could barely walk with a cane. She couldn't follow her son to the door any longer. She would yell for him to close the door loud enough so that she could hear the door slam shut. She wanted to make sure he was outside before she forced herself to get up to get the coins he would need for their provisions. After she was up and in the kitchen, she would scream, "And don't come in until I call you!" The more her son did for her, the stingier she became.

Felipe was approaching middle age, and now life seemed unbearable. His mother resented that she could barely move, so all she did was nag. She would complain about the food, complain about the house and yell and scream at her son all day long and even into the night when she couldn't sleep. What was he to do?

Felipe would often think of that happy day when he held the money from the sale of the farm animals. What is it about money that is magic to people? He started to think money would be the answer to all his problems. His mother always kept the kitchen windows covered with black cloth, and she never allowed him in the kitchen without her. The money had to be hidden there, he thought.

On a cold and dreary day, the exasperated son came up with a sinister plan. His mother sent him out of the house as she always did, but this time he slammed the door as she expected and then snuck over and hid behind the pantry door. A moment later, his unsuspecting mother hobbled by using her cane to help her walk. She walked over to the kitchen sink, which had a hand pump to draw water from a pipe that reached deep down into an underground well. She stooped down and opened the hinged doors that covered the bottom of the sink, and after searching under the floorboards around the pipe, she struggled to pull up a heavy sack. Felipe was amazed that the money gave his mother the strength to do all this. That money was really powerful. His curiosity caused him to lean against the pantry door to get a better look. The door made a tiny squeak, but Sinforosa's keen ears picked up the sound.

Sinforosa took on the look of a wild and deadly animal that uses its senses to detect and attack its predator. She set the sack of coins down and turned toward the pantry. She began to walk without the use of the cane but carried the cane as if it were a weapon. Felipe trembled while thinking about what to do if he were discovered. He envisioned himself being beaten and locked up in a closet. In those few seconds, all kinds of horrible things went through his mind, stemming from his childhood memories. He began to sweat and shiver in fear. As the door was violently opened, his eyes bulged, his face turned red and he began to scream like someone who had gone mad. Felipe charged forward, throwing Sinforosa flat on the floor. In shock, he stopped to see his mother's lifeless body. Was this a trick? Would the beast jump up to devour its prey?

Felipe found the courage to carefully move closer. For the first time in a very long, long time, the house was totally silent. His mother did not make a sound. He took her hand to remove the cane, but she held on to it with a deadly grasp. Unexpectedly, he fell forward. Lying face to face with his mother, Felipe expected the worse, but still she did not move. She did not take a breath. His mother was dead. Felipe calmly lifted himself up. For the first time, he felt free.

Felipe didn't cry for his mother. He didn't even have remorse. He checked the heavy bag. It was filled with gold coins. He looked under the floorboards, and far beneath on the ground below, filled to capacity, were bags and bags of money. He jumped for joy, forgetting all about his mother. The delighted son decided to take the bags of valuable coins and bury them deep in the ground beside a large boulder near the house. After he finished, he sat down on the large rock to think. What would he do with his mother? The villagers would wonder how she had died. If he told them how it happened, would they believe him? Would the villagers accuse him of killing her? Then he remembered the money. The villagers would want to know why he had been hiding in the pantry, and then he would have to tell them about the money. If there was something his parents did do right, it was to keep the money a secret. He knew instinctively that if anyone found out about the money, they would take it from him.

It didn't take Felipe long to come up with an idea. He decided to go to the cemetery, which was over the hill just a mile away. He would bury his mother in the same grave with his father. After all, "two peas in a pod belong together." By the time the villagers got suspicious, he would live in a place far away. The disturbed man thought of living happily ever after with his bags of silver and gold coins. So off to the cemetery he went and began to dig. The tired son stopped. He could see the skull and what looked like his father's arms. Felipe remembered there was no coffin. The startled man quickly went to pick up his mother's body from home. By the time Felipe got home, it was already getting dark. He quickly went into the kitchen and picked her up. She was very heavy. The weary son could barely carry her. Felipe would have to use the wagon, even if there was no horse. Pulling the wagon would be easier than carrying her all that way.

Felipe went to the cemetery pulling the wagon in the moonlight. When he got to the grave, he looked in and was frightened to see the skull of his father uncovered. The black holes of his eyes stared right up at him. Even more frightening than his skull were his outstretched arms, which reached straight up from the dirt as if waiting to grasp someone. Terrorized, Felipe began to talk to himself, "There was a little wind earlier, and the wind blew some of the dirt away."

Felipe walked over to his mother. He almost screamed. Her eyes were opened wide, and for a moment he was convinced his mother had not died. "Mother, please, don't be angry. I thought you were dead!" Felipe cried. He waited for her to hit him or something, but she did nothing. "You are dead. You can't hurt me!" he yelled. "What is wrong with me? I'm tired! I'm just tired! I'm imagining things." He reached over to pick her up, but no matter how hard he tried, he could not lift her. "Come on, Mother, Father is waiting for you," Felipe urged. Still, he could not pick her up. Felipe turned around and pulled her arms around his neck to pull her up with his back. He finally moved her and struggled over to the grave.

Felipe tried to get his mother off of his back, but her arms wouldn't budge. Her hands were tightly clasped together in a very mysterious hold. Horrified, Felipe swung his mother, trying to shake her off. But no matter what he did, she still clung to him. Then he heard someone laugh. "Father, is that you?" he asked. His father never laughed. Bad memories came rushing into his head. Yes, his father had laughed once. He was just a little boy when a giant snake had suddenly appeared in the yard, and he began to cry. His father had yelled, "Stop crying and pick up the snake and kill it." Felipe, petrified, could not move. Andres picked up the snake and used it as a whip.

He laughed as the boy ran wildly around the yard trying to escape the lash of the snake. Felipe was quickly brought to the present as the laughter of his father became louder in his mind. In a mad panic, he ran with his mother attached to his back in a deathly grip.

If you wander off near Arroyo Hondo on a moonlit night, they say you can see the ghost of this sorrowful son who is forever traveling over the hills with his mother clinging to his back. It is also said that if you see a ball of fire floating mysteriously over the rocks, it will lead you to where the treasure of gold and silver coins is buried.

## Juan Goche

*Vida sin amigos, muerte sin testigos.*
Life without friends, death without witnesses.

They say Juan was a brawny man with strong arms and shoulders who could do the work of ten men. This man, along with the other men of the nearby *haciendas* and *ranchos*, helped dig and maintain the string of ditches that channeled off from the Rio Grande to the fields surrounding the villages. It was a hard job, but once the work was done and they could see the fruits of their labor as the water flowed along irrigating the fields, it brought a deep sense of satisfaction. Ditch work in those days was a special trade. Juan Goche loved the work, and it was all he lived for.

Juan hadn't always just thought about ditch digging. He had loved going to the yearly *fiesta* of Tomé. He was always one of the first at the *matanza*, the slaughter of a pig to make all sorts of delicious pig's meat things to eat. During the fiesta, he could eat, drink and be merry. He enjoyed drinking the wine that people made from the grapes grown in the nearby fields. He also liked seeing the *rodeos* and the Corridas del Gallo. These were actual horse races in which the young men of the villages competed. A rooster would be buried in the ground with only its head showing. Those competing in the race would line up their horses along a two- or three-inch-deep line that would be scratched into the ground with a stick. At the sound of a gunshot, they would all take off in a mad dash to try to reach the rooster first. At that point, they would have to ride sidesaddle, reaching down and pulling the rooster right out of the ground. The man carrying the rooster to the finish line would win the contest.

Back in the early days, who do you think would always win? Juan Goche, of course. He had this big strong horse named Lightning that could take off

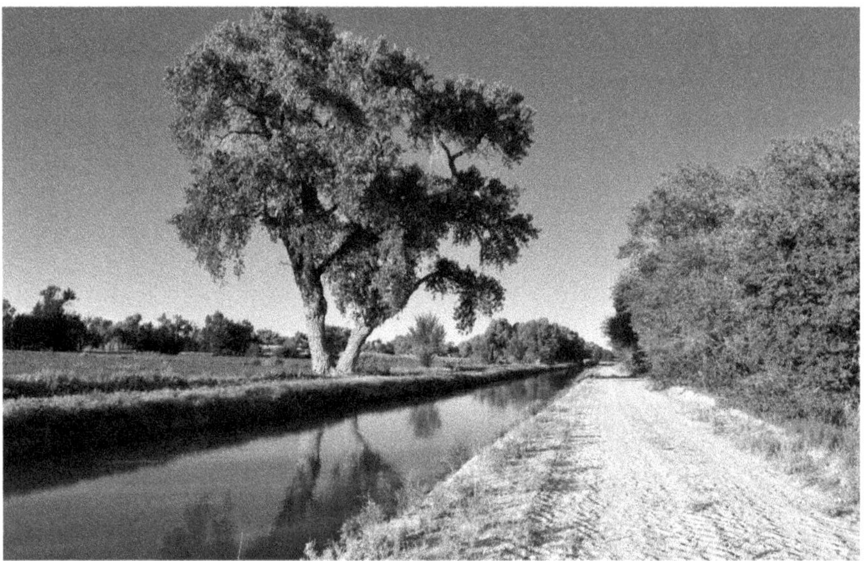

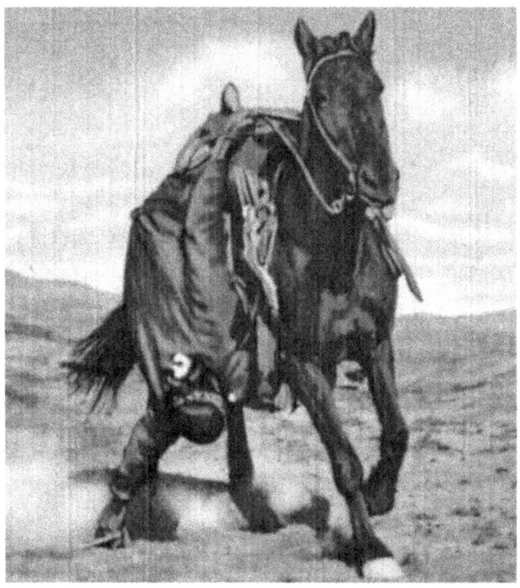

*Above*: "Acequia," photograph. *©2010 Ramon Juan Carlos de Aragón.*

*Left*: *Corrida del Gallo*, Genuine Curtech-Chicago, C.T. Art-Colortone, distributed by J.R. Willis, Albuquerque, NM, circa 1945. *Author's collection.*

in a flash and leave all of the other horses biting his dust. Juan Goche would always smile when he remembered the time he went to a fandango at the conclusion of the fiesta at Don Miguel Baca's *sala*. The dance hall had these huge wooden double doors. The hall also had high ceilings, which were typical in those days. Juan Goche decided to ride his horse into the sala when people were dancing. You should have heard the people yelling as he rode around inside the building. They all ran out until Juan Goche was the only one left.

Juan Goche married Alicia Vallejos, whom he had known since childhood. She also loved the Tomé fiestas. They had three daughters, which did not make him very happy. He had always wanted a son. His daughters were as squeamish as their mother at the cockfights called *Las Peleas del Gallo.* Juan took extra special care of Colorado because the strong bird was his winning rooster. The cockfights and races were a tradition in New Mexico dating back to the Spanish colonial days. It was a sporting event that some people liked but others didn't.

More than all these things and even his family, he loved to work with the *acequias* (irrigation canals). Ditches came in all sizes, and Juan Goche knew them inside and out. He was an expert in acequias, and he became quite well known throughout the land. They talked about him in Adelino, Jarales and even as far down south as Mesilla. He was rather famous in his day and age.

The alcalde of Tomé appointed Juan Goche as a *patron del agua*, a water master. As a water master, he would get up at the crack of dawn every morning, saddle his horse and ride along the miles and miles of ditches, checking them. Sometimes, late at night, people could still see him riding along the ditch banks in the moonlight.

Being a water master was the highest position to which anyone in the farmlands and valleys could aspire. This was especially true in the *Rio Abajo*, the lower Rio Grande Valley, near the Isleta Indian Pueblo where relations between the Indians and the Spanish had been friendly for generations. Juan Goche had to go to the chief of Isleta to ask for water to be released from the Gran Atarque, the great dam that the Indians controlled. Water masters had a lot of power and control. They could say who could get water and who could not.

Needless to say, Alicia and her three daughters hardly ever saw Juan. He was happy with his acequias, and he didn't seem to need anything or anyone. One day, he came home and his family was gone. Some say Alicia simply got tired of taking care of the farm on her own. Juan made good money, so she hired a ranch hand to help out. She saved a great deal of money in the bank. When Alicia and her daughters left with the ranch hand, she withdrew the money and left Juan with nothing. She even sold the chickens and his pig, called Gordo. Juan never heard from them again.

One day, the water master decided to move from his adobe home in the village. He decided to live in a house he built with branches, twigs and mud near El Seno, which was the largest canal. It was more like a dugout. It had a little hole in the roof so the smoke could go out when he was cooking or heating his little home. He would sit for hours in his dugout wondering

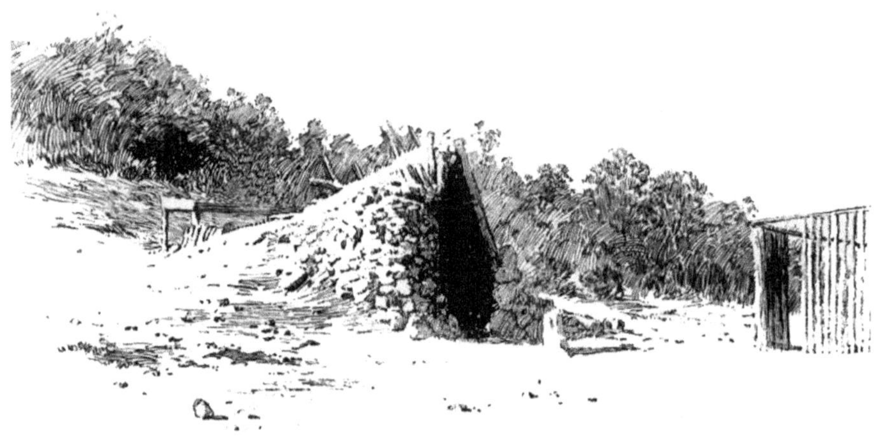

*A dugout.* From F.M. Endlich, "The Heart of New Mexico," *Harper's Weekly*, supplement, September 7, 1889. *Author's collection.*

why people just didn't understand they could not water unless it was their turn. Didn't they know what a mess it would cause for everyone else who was scheduled to water after them? The chaos that resulted enraged Juan. He had to explain to the angry farmers waiting for the precious water that others had overwatered their fields. Then they argued that maybe he should be replaced as the water master if he didn't know how to do his job. If he had to live near the main canal the rest of his life just to make sure everyone was following orders, that is what he would do!

As the winters passed by, Juan Goche got very old and very weary. He even failed to go into the village to buy his provisions. He could no longer do the work of ten men. He couldn't even do the work of one. His muscles ached all of the time, and he could only watch as the younger men cleaned and maintained the ditches. He would yell at them and stomp his feet, telling them they weren't doing the work right. "Back in my day," he would say, "I could do the work of fifty men. I could handle everything! Nobody had to tell me anything because I knew how to do it." Juan Goche went from being a popular man of legend to one people feared because of his ranting and raving. He became a crotchety old man.

The kids were always playing in the ditches. When he chased them away, they laughed and made fun of him. Now, kids back in those days were typical kids like they are today. They loved playing in the ditch water. Sometimes they would wade across a ditch to get to the other side. Other times, they would jump up and down and splash one another when the water was shallow. They had great fun in the water, not realizing it could be very dangerous.

They looked out for Juan Goche, and when they didn't see him, they would run to the ditches. The old water master had an eagle eye, however. He was always on the lookout trying to spot them.

The situation with the kids playing in the water got so bad that the water master decided to come up with a plan. He got this great big gunnysack that he used to carry things and swung it over his shoulder. He went from farms to ranches warning everyone to keep the children away from the ditches. He would say, "You never know, someone could pick them up. That would be a terrible thing." His warnings seemed like threats. Were they threats, or was he just concerned for their safety? Soon, people began telling stories that they could hear something like the sound of cats screeching, pulling and tugging from inside Juan Goche's sack. But then, it wasn't like the sound of cats. What was it? Was it just their imagination, or did it sound like crying, whimpering children trying to get out?

People thought Juan Goche had finally gone crazy. It got to the point where no one would have anything at all to do with him. He was very lonely, but no one cared. He complained, but no one listened. Juan Goche was a bitter old man who had lost his family, his friends and even the work he loved. They occasionally caught a glimpse of him walking along the ditch banks with a full sack over his shoulder. Just when people started to believe he must have died, someone would say they thought they had seen him walking along the banks. These sightings of Juan Goche guarding the waters of the ditches went on for generations. No one really knows how long he lived or if he's still living.

## Gold Teeth

*Donde lloran esta La Muerte.*
Where there is death there is crying.

Life in nineteenth-century New Mexico was very different from what it is today. People worked hard, and families shared folk stories or went to fandangos for entertainment. This story begins with Pedro and Elena, a young couple very much in love. Pedro was born on a ranch on the plains, and Elena had always lived by the Old Town Plaza in Las Vegas. In other words, Pedro was a country boy, and Elena was a city girl. But they both had something in common: they had families who loved them very much.

Pedro was handsome and polite and always had a smile on his face. He didn't talk much and was really quite shy. He lost his father at the age of four.

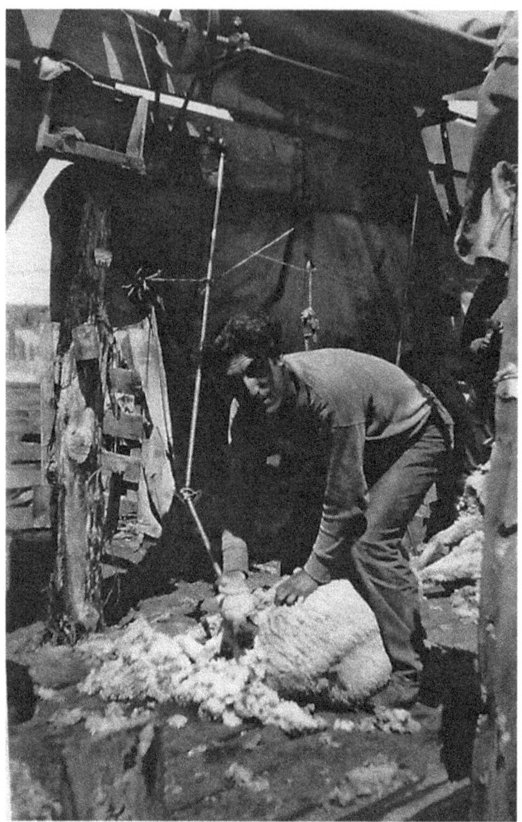

Sheepshearing in a New Mexico sheep ranch; unknown date and location. *Author's collection.*

He had fond memories of ringing the large bell outside their home when it was time for his father to come in from the fields to eat. He was still too young to help his father, but his father would tell him each day when he left the house that he had a very important job to do at home, and that was to take care of his beautiful mother while he was away at work. One evening, Pedro rang and rang the bell, but his father never came. He and his mother went out to look for his dad. They found him lying on the ground, dead. Some say it was his bad heart that killed him, just as his father before him. Pedro took care of his mother, whom he also loved very much, until her death when he turned twenty-five. He was very happy on the ranch on his own and rarely went into the city. Until one day he met Elena at a fandango.

Elena was beautiful and sociable and enjoyed dancing and singing. When she walked into a room, she was often accompanied by many friends, and her contagious laughter and talking could be heard everywhere. When Pedro and Elena met, it was love at first sight. Soon, Pedro asked Elena to marry him.

The young couple got married at the Nuestra Señora de Los Dolores Church in Las Vegas, and they had a big dance and reception at the plaza. After the wedding feast, Pedro took Elena out to his ranch. It was a nice ranch with a pond full of fish, a pasture with cattle that grazed happily as the birds flew chirping overhead and chickens in a coop that laid fresh eggs every morning. The ranch also had a nice garden with ripe, juicy vegetables and an outdoor oven, which they called a *horno*, to bake sweet-smelling bread.

Even though Elena had grown up in the city, she fit right into this place. She learned to cook and sew and to take care of the house. She canned and dried vegetables and fruit and made jam and *carne seca*, jerky, for the winter months. They were both very happy. Pedro would rise with the crow of the roosters and head straight to work on mending the fences and feeding the cows and horses. Elena would ring the bell whenever she needed him or to remind him it was time to eat. In the beginning, it was all new and exciting for Elena.

The ranch on the plains was pretty far from Las Vegas, and little by little Elena's friends and family stopped going out to see her. Her elderly parents came out to the ranch to visit as often as they could, but their health was failing and the trip was hard. Elena would go to town with her husband whenever they needed to buy the things they couldn't grow or make on the farm. Elena missed her social life. She would occasionally convince Pedro to take her to the fandangos, but not as often as she would have liked. Pedro was happy just to have her to himself, and their solitude at the ranch was pleasant enough for him, although they often talked about having children. The first year went by and then the second and the third. Elena was beginning to think they would never have a child. She spent most of her time working and alone. This made her angry at times. If she could have a child, she would have someone to play with and talk to. Still, no children came.

Then one morning, just as Pedro was getting ready to leave to feed the animals, Elena let out a horrible scream. Pedro rushed into the house. He found his beautiful wife lying on the floor with blood flowing out of her mouth. She had been trying to place a heavy iron skillet on the warmer above the wood stove when it slid out of her hands, bounced off the stove and smashed into her mouth. The skillet knocked out Elena's teeth.

Pedro put Elena in the buckboard and took her straight into town, where the doctor did the best he could. He pulled and yanked out all of the little daggers of teeth that could be extracted from her injured gums. Elena preferred that Pedro stay on the farm while she was recovering at her parents' home. She could not stand for him to look at her. She couldn't help but feel that somehow it was his fault. She wanted to stay with her parents until she was healed. It would bring her mother to tears to watch her beautiful daughter suffer. Elena cried all the time. She had to return to the dentist for several days to endure more torture. She was taking so much pain medicine that at times she didn't know where she was. She slept most of the time. One morning, Elena's father went into her room to give her more bad news. "Your mother died in her sleep last night," he told her. Elena could not cry or say anything. She just lay in her bed staring at her father, numb from the medicine.

Elena would eat very little, and her father stopped eating, too. He missed his wife, and he felt as if he had lost his daughter as well. One day, Pedro stopped in to see how Elena was doing. Elena was asleep. Her medicine bottle was empty. Her father sat in his chair, his head back and his eyes closed. Pedro tried to speak to his father-in-law, but there was no response. When he reached out to awaken him, his head slumped over. He felt cold. He was dead.

Pedro returned to the ranch, and this time his wife was with him. Most of the time, she just slept. Pedro was in such despair that he didn't know what to do. He cooked, cleaned and took care of the ranch. One day, Pedro decided to pay a visit to Dr. Demarest, the country doctor, to explain the situation to him. Dr. Demarest carefully listened and came up with an idea. He told Pedro to go across the street and see Roberto Leyba, the silver and gold smith. Pedro was willing to try anything.

Roberto Leyba listened as Pedro told him about his problem. Then, Leyba smiled and said, "I think I can help you, my friend." He led Pedro into a room where he had a glass showcase filled with dentures. He had dentures carved out of wood and bone. He also had some made with silver and gold. "This could be the answer to all of your problems," Leyba beamed. "Which set do you like?"

It didn't take Pedro long to choose a set of gold dentures in the dark corner of the showcase. "You made a very good choice," Roberto Leyba said. But he failed to tell Pedro that an old widow named Doña Josefa had had that set made especially for her. She really loved her dentures and didn't want to part with them. But Doña Josefa had recently passed away, and her daughter felt it was a waste of money to bury such beautiful gold teeth with her mother. She sold the dentures back to the jeweler. The jeweler agreed. They were a work of art and much too beautiful to be buried with the dead.

Leyba put the dentures in a beautiful glass box and then covered the box with gold paper and a pretty lavender ribbon. Pedro was anxious to see his wife's reaction to the gift. He handed the box to Elena. She just looked at the box but wouldn't open it. He pulled on the lavender ribbon, and the gold paper opened up, exposing a glass box with the gold teeth inside. Elena was finally curious. After a moment, she removed the glass lid, took out the dentures, held them close to her face and half smiled. This was the most expression Pedro had seen from Elena in a very long time. "Try them on," Pedro said excitedly. "Aren't they beautiful?" he added.

Elena stood up, not saying a word. She walked slowly to the mirror and popped the gold dentures into her mouth. She finally gave a big smile as she saw the shiny teeth gleaming and radiant in the light. "Do you like them?" he asked.

"Who are you?" Elena responded in a strange voice as she turned toward Pedro.

"Your husband, of course," he said.

"I don't believe I've had a husband in a very long time," she stated.

"I'm so sorry if you feel that way, Elena. I've tried the best I can to help you through all of this," Pedro answered.

"Please, go outside and make yourself useful, young man," Elena said. "I've got to get some rest."

Pedro was confused. He hadn't expected this, and it wasn't exactly as he had hoped for, but anything was better than how things had been—or so he thought.

Days went by, and Elena still wasn't herself, but at least she baked and cooked and sometimes tidied up the house. She loved to eat. Elena started to put on some of the weight she had lost. She talked so vividly about people and things from long ago as if she had been there that Pedro wondered how she could know so much. Elena seemed very happy most of the time. She never asked to go anywhere. She was content just staying alone in the house.

Time passed, and things were going pretty well. One day, after an especially good day, Elena seemed to be in a very good mood. Pedro got the courage to ask her a question that had been on his mind for a while. "I know I started sleeping in the barn, but you seem to be so much better now that we should consider my moving back into our bedroom. Maybe you would like to think about having the baby you always wanted?"

At first, Elena just looked at him with surprise, and then she picked up the broom, which was nearby. "Now listen here, young man. I don't know who you think you are, but don't think for one minute that I'm going to allow you into my bed. And as for children, well, I can assure you that one daughter was quite enough. She was a horrible little thing who took everything away from me." Elena began to wave her broom in the air, yelling for him to get out of the house.

Pedro tried to reason with her. "But, Elena, please…I'm sorry…we can wait for as long as you want. I'm just so happy you are feeling well again."

However, Elena just got angrier and angrier and yelled at him, "Get out! Get out of my house!"

Pedro worried about what to do next. Elena was no longer the girl he had married. She aged before his eyes, and she spoke to him as if he were a stranger. She bossed him around and constantly told him what to do, and now she had thrown him out of his own home. This could not be right! After all, he had been born and raised there. His home had belonged to his father and his grandfather before him. Pedro loved Elena, but this woman Elena had become was not the one he wanted to spend the rest of his life with. Then he thought about something. Elena had begun to feel better with the gold dentures, but for some strange reason they had changed her. He didn't care if Elena had teeth or not, or what she looked like. All he wanted was the woman who had once loved him. He made a plan to sneak into the house after Elena was asleep and steal the golden teeth.

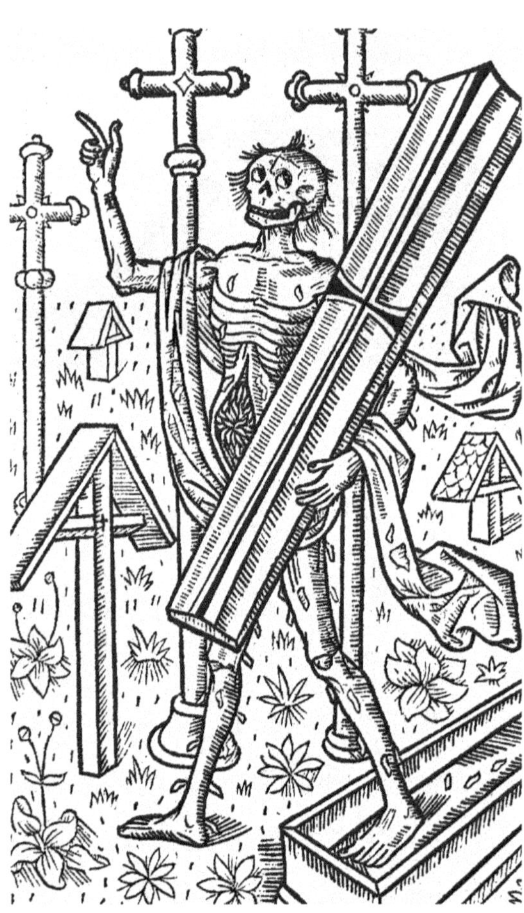

Allegoric representation of Death. From "Le grant kalendrier et compost des Bergiers," printed by Nicolas le Rouge, Troyes, 1496. *Author's collection.*

It was finally nighttime. Pedro waited until the lights went out. He got into the house easily. He walked slowly and quietly. As he neared the bedroom where Elena slept, he could hear her snoring. He peeked in through the bedroom door. She was lying on her back. On the little table next to the bed was the glass box that held the gold dentures. The teeth suddenly began to clatter as Pedro crept in. Elena instinctively moved her hand over the glass box, as if to comfort the teeth. She was still in a deep, deep sleep. Pedro waited for a second and then took the glass box, tiptoed out of the room and ran out of the house. As he ran, the bell outside began to ring. He wondered if he should return, but instead, he got on his horse and rode all the way into town until he got to Leyba's shop. Pedro felt so tired that he could barely keep his eyes open, even with the clatter coming from the teeth. They were going wild. "How can I silence them?" he asked himself. "I will sit on the glass box while I rest."

To Pedro's amazement, the sound stopped, and he fell into an uneasy sleep.

Pedro was awakened by the sound of a bell ringing and someone distantly calling his name. At first, it seemed as if it was Elena calling to him, but as the voice grew steadily louder, he wasn't sure. "Pedroooo, Pedrooo," he heard as it got menacingly closer. Without warning, he heard footsteps and then dead silence. A movement nearby brought terror to his eyes when he saw a black figure in the moonlight. There, near him, stood an old woman with wild white hair and piercing red eyes. "Where are my gold teeth?" she cried.

Pedro felt a sharp pain in his chest. He couldn't talk.

"I want my gold teeth!" she screamed.

Pedro became motionless. The dreadful woman grabbed him and shook him. "Where are my gold teeth?"

The townspeople heard screams but were too afraid to leave their homes until morning. Pedro was found dead, sitting up against a wall, and the decaying corpse of a long-dead woman was next to him with the gold teeth in her smiling skull. They say Pedro died of a heart attack; as for Elena, she was never seen or heard from again.

## The Legend of La Pavura Blanca

*El que al Camposanto va al Camposanto llega.*
If you seek death, death will find you.

It was a bright, beautiful sunny day filled with the thrill of adventure when the grand Coronado expedition was to set forth from Compostela, a town located five hundred miles northwest of the capital of New Spain, Mexico City. The group was to search for the Seven Cities of Cibola, a land, according to ancient Indian lore, filled with turquoise and gold.

Francisca de Hozes, the wife of Alonso Sanchez, simply couldn't contain herself as she talked to her friend Manuela de Godoy. Manuela was betrothed to Alonso's cousin, Hernando de Luna. "This is so exciting, Manuela. You're going to have the grandest wedding when you marry Hernando!"

"I wish I could go, too. I don't want to stay behind waiting," Manuela responded.

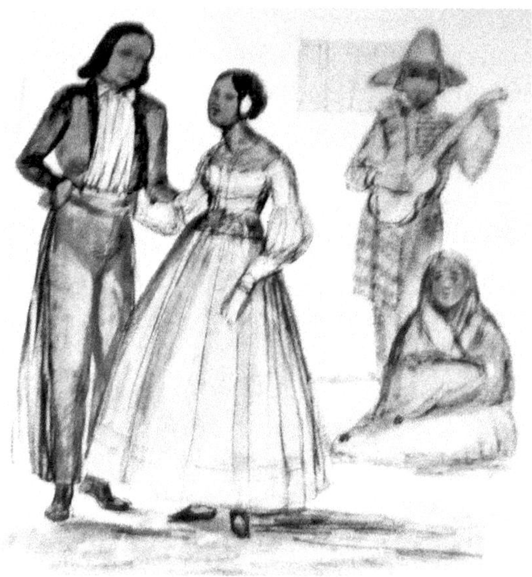

Fandango illustration by J.W. Abert, 1846–47, from his travel diary as he journeyed through New Mexico with the American military writing about and illustrating what he saw. *Author's collection.*

"Oh, no!" Francisca exclaimed. "You can't even think of it!"

Captain General Don Francisco Vásquez de Coronado y Luján only allowed a few of the wives of the soldiers to go along. "Once you and Hernando are married, there will be plenty of chances for the two of you to go out on other grand adventures." It was natural that Manuela should be worried. Quite often, young Spanish explorers were taking their lives in their own hands when venturing off into unknown and unexplored lands.

On February 22, 1540, the feast day of Santa Margarita de Cortona, patroness of charity and protectoress of the eyes, everyone who was going on the journey went to confession heard by the pious Franciscan frays. All of the adventurers went to Holy Mass and prayed deeply to Santa Margarita, the Holy Trinity and the Virgin Mary for a safe journey. You should have heard the clatter and noise of the oxen-pulled wooden carts; the horses, stallions and mares; the lances, harquebus, cannons; and the men and women who went back and forth loading things up. It was quite a sight to behold, with hundreds of people preparing and leaving for a spectacular journey of discovery that might lead to a new life of wealth and prosperity for all. But the most eye-catching sight were the two lovebirds, Manuela de Godoy and Hernando de Luna. It seemed as though they were inseparable, but Hernando promised Manuela that they would live a life of comfort and happiness forever upon his return.

"You promise?" Manuela asked Hernando as she kissed him one last time.

"Yes, I do," he answered as he held her tightly. "You know I love you. I would follow you to the ends of the earth!"

"And I will always follow you," Manuela replied. She cried and watched as the expedition departed and did not move from where she stood until she could no longer distinguish them from the distant horizon.

It turned out that the journey for the Coronado expedition was much harder than expected. Following an ancient Indian trail the Spanish would eventually call El Camino Real, the hardy travelers encountered flat, dry country; horrendous winds; and very strong, sudden rains, plus rattlesnakes, poisonous plants and scorpions. Needless to say, some of the explorers died from exposure and thirst. The site where a person died was considered sacred by the Spanish, so these places were marked with crosses and called *pasajes del difunto* (passageways of the deceased), meaning where the soul went on to another world. Now we call these sites *descansos* (resting places), but in the past, descansos were actually spots marked with crosses and piled up with stones where a funeral procession carrying a coffin would stop, set the coffin down, rest and pray before proceeding on to the cemetery. It depended on how many miles the cemetery was from the deceased's house how many descansos there were. At the very beginning, there were no cemeteries for the Spanish, of course, so they simply looked for a good spot to bury the bodies, and these sites were also marked with crosses.

It is believed that the unfortunate group of explorers at one point passed near an area called the White Sands. This is an unusual natural wonder where white gypsum from the surrounding mountains dissolves and is carried by runoff waters into a huge basin measuring countless numbers of miles. Resulting white gypsum dunes are sometimes forty or fifty feet high, and like sand deserts, the dunes continue to grow through the forces of nature.

According to legend, somewhere near there, marauding Indians attacked members of the Coronado expedition. In this group was Hernando de Luna. It isn't known whether he was kidnapped or killed by the Indians, or if he lost his way in the dunes after a sandstorm. The spot where he disappeared and two others were killed was marked with three crosses. Coronado and his group of brave explorers never found the Cities of Gold. His expedition failed, but he managed to explore, map and document unknown territories that no European had ever set sight on before. It was quite a remarkable accomplishment, but the explorers returned to Compostela disappointed and forlorn.

News traveled quickly, and people gathered in the plaza to wait for the arrival of the travelers. Manuela rushed into town, but she couldn't wait. She joined some of the others who were preparing their horses to ride out to welcome the explorers home. Upon meeting the distraught travelers, the group quickly told stories of what had happened on the expedition. Manuela de Godoy only wanted to hear about Hernando. "Where is he? Why did they leave him behind?" she asked herself when she discovered that he wasn't with them. She broke down in a stream of tears upon hearing that the love of her life could be gone forever. "He must be alive," she thought. "Where is his body?"

No one had actually seen him die. This brought her hope. "I know he's alive. He is probably wounded or hurt and waiting for me. Hernando knows I would never fail him, just as I know he would never leave me waiting."

Manuela de Godoy recalled the promise Hernando had made as he rode away: "I will return, and we will never be apart again."

"I will search for him until I find him, even if it takes me to the ends of the earth," she told Francisca.

"Oh God, please keep your senses!" Francisca pleaded.

But Manuela wouldn't listen. She stubbornly packed food and clothing, saddled her horse and rode off like the wind, leaving the dust behind her. No one could change her mind or stop her from leaving. The poor girl rode fiercely for days and nights, stopping only to give her horse a little rest and water until she reached the White Sands. When Manuela de Godoy finally got to the dunes, she dismounted her worn and weary horse. Determined and hopeful, Manuela walked tirelessly as her faithful horse followed. She ran out of water. The heat was unbearable during the day, but at night the haunting winds were bitter cold. In a blinding sandstorm, her horse disappeared, but her unwavering hope that Hernando was alive kept her going.

Lost and alone, fueled by her love in search of the man she could not bear to live without, Manuela de Godoy moved slowly and desperately through the White Sands. The intrepid explorers described the three crosses they had placed to mark the last resting place of those they lost in the whiteness of the dunes shortly before a disastrous storm. Some of their group had died, and they were buried, but the relentless wind had quickly erased their graves with waves of endless white sand. In the moonlight, Manuela noticed some dark forms that appeared like crosses against the whiteness of the sand. With wishful eyes, Manuela saw what appeared to her to be three men walking over and under the dunes. With a burst of strength, she ran toward them. They were nearby yet so far away.

"Hernando, here I am. I knew you would find me!" poor Manuela cried out. No sooner would she climb over one sand dune then she would see them going over another. She frantically shouted at the top of her lungs for Hernando, but he could not hear her. "My Hernando, it has to be my

Hernando," Manuela thought. At times, she believed she could hear his voice calling out to her. It encouraged her to move on. She felt he was getting closer. She would fall, pick herself up and keep on going. She died somewhere there in the white desert, *La Pavura Blanca*.

The Pavura Blanca are the dreadful and terror-filled eddies of white dust that unmercifully cover those who stray into its white blanket during windswept cold and forlorn moonlit nights. If brave souls should venture forth on the White Sands during certain forbidding nights, chances are that they will see the spirit of Manuela de Godoy. Some say if you stay very quiet and still, you will hear the echo of Hernando's name coming from the lips of his beloved. Others, who are more romantic, will say the spirits of Manuela and Hernando found each other in the rolling dunes. Their joyful laughter travels with the breeze throughout the White Sands as a reminder of an unbroken promise to be with each other in love and happiness for all eternity.

## Juana Marchanta

*La envidia mata.*
Envy kills.

There was something very special about the little girl who was born in Peñasco near Taos to Don Felipe Madrid and Doña Ana Chavez de Madrid on December 25, 1820. Her godparents, Don Severino Martinez and Doña María del Carmel Santistevan, christened her Juana María. As was the custom for generations in New Mexico, she also received the name María. This was because it was believed that every single Hispana newborn girl's life had to be dedicated to the blessed mother of Jesus. As was also the tradition, her father promised Juana in marriage to the son of his neighbor, Don Julian Abeyta. Don Julian's son was already eleven years old, but when Juana would be of marriageable age, she would have to marry Diego Abeyta. Arranged marriages were a medieval custom from Spain. Sometimes they were done to unite the landholdings and personal wealth of two families. Such was the case for Juana's parents.

Juana María Madrid spent many hours learning from her nana, Doña Josefita, who also lived with them. Her nana knew all of the *dichos* and had a dicho for every day, so little Juana learned many of the sayings of her culture. She also helped her mother and grandmother prepare all of the meals. Juana could bake bread in the *horno* like her ancestors had done

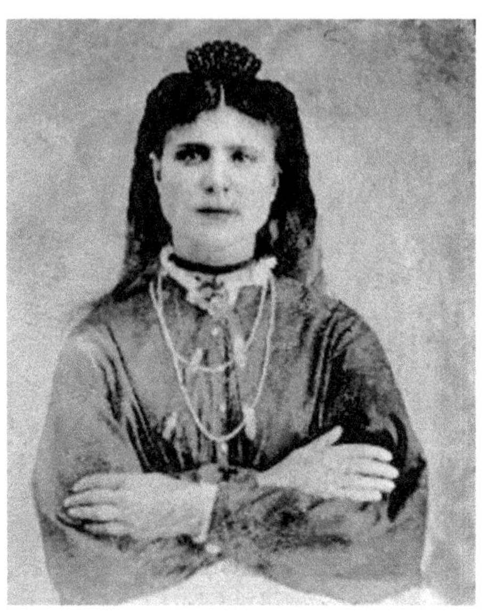

Tintype, circa 1860. *Author's collection.*

in Spain for centuries, and she learned the Spanish traditional stories of enchanted castles, princesses, monsters and witches. By 1826, when Juana was six years old, news spread about a new school opening in Taos.

Padre Antonio José Martinez, the pastor of Our Lady of Guadalupe Church, opened the school. Padre Martinez was the son of Juana's godparents. Don Felipe decided to let his sons Armando and Tranquilino, whom they called "Lino," attend the school. Armando and Lino were older than Juana. Don Felipe had gone into Taos to talk to Padre Martinez. The good padre told him that he was setting up a dormitory for the students who lived too far away to ride horseback to school every day. Don Felipe discussed it with his wife. School would be three days a week for ten hours a day. Homework would be assigned, the priest said, but it would not interfere with farm work. Don Felipe and Doña Ana both agreed that it would be a good thing for their sons. Juana pleaded with her parents to be allowed to go to school, too.

The padre said in his announcements that the new Our Lady of Guadalupe School would be for both boys and girls, so Juana had a good case. After much discussion, Juana was allowed to go to the school. She would be housed in a separate room with other girls at night and cared for when not in the classroom by María Teodora Romero, who was the priest's housekeeper.

Teodora worked for the padre not only as his housekeeper but also helping him operate his orphanage to care for *espositos*, unwanted foundlings left at the church. The padre had a good heart, so he raised many abandoned infants and children and adopted them as his own according to the religious and civil laws of the time. Some of the children required constant care. Juana got involved with everything at the school and the orphanage from the first day. There were at least thirty kids of all ages sitting on wooden benches in a long room. Juana was the youngest at six. The girls sat in the front and the boys in the back. There were kids from all over northern New Mexico. All of the boys and girls were eager to learn.

Juana listened carefully as the enthusiastic padre explained everything they would learn. He talked about reading, writing, spelling, arithmetic and learning about their faith and about all the arts. They would get to perform in plays and in a passion play the priest himself had written. They sang and danced and made musical instruments for recreation. On special days, they carved *santos* and learned to paint *retablos*. School would be hard work but also fun, even though it would be year round.

As the days, weeks and months passed by, one of the favorite things Juana liked to do was write poetry. Padre Martinez was noted as a *poeta*, someone who could compose sonnets, lyric poems, odes, epic poems and verses for songs. One day in 1827, Don Trinidad Barceló, the superintendent of education for New Mexico, made a visit to the school. He was impressed with all the boys and girls who sang and danced for him and gave him some gifts they had made. Juana would often sing *cuandos* (ballads) about her experiences at school. On one solemn occasion, she wrote a cuando about the man, Diego Abeyta, whom her father had promised she would marry when she was of age. Don Julian's son had died suddenly in a tragic accident on the farm. The community came together as it always did on such occasions to mourn with the family. Juana never questioned that she would be Diego's wife. It was part of their culture, and she never doubted the wisdom of tradition, but she felt there was something more she was being called to do. Juana pleaded with her father to not promise her in marriage to anyone. She had to think and decide what her plans for the future would be. Continuing her education was certainly something she had to do.

One of the most exciting events for the school and the community took place in 1835, when Padre Martinez arrived back home from a trip to the capital city of Santa Fé. Juana was now a young lady of fifteen. The priest had purchased a printing press that had been brought all the way from Mexico along the El Camino Real to Santa Fé. The padre even hired its operator, Jesus María Baca, because he wanted all his students to learn how to use it. The padre had founded Our Lady of Guadalupe Seminary for the training of boys to study for the priesthood in 1833. Some of the other priests helped him with his seminary and the school. Both his school and his seminary had more students each year.

Once home, Juana had to copy and learn to sing the alabados in praise of the cross during processions and special feast days. Her mother and grandmother belonged to the Carmelitas and were also members of *Las*

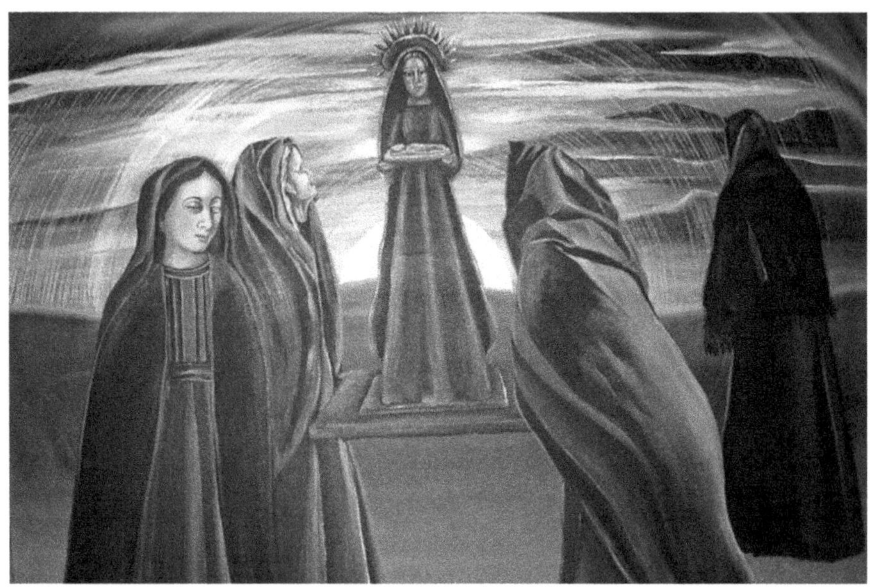

*Carmelitas*, acrylic on canvas painting. *©2010 Rosa María Calles.*

*Hermanas de la Santísima Cruz*. The Sisters of the Holy Cross was a Spanish colonial laywomen's order in New Mexico that was dedicated to honoring and promoting the veneration of the cross and crucifix. They hoped Juana would also choose to become a member, but it would be her choice.

Juana began to see the injustices against women. It didn't matter how intelligent a woman was, she was never at the same level as a man. She admired her teacher, Padre Martinez, for his immense knowledge in every branch of education. The padre had studied to become a priest at the Tridentine Seminary under the See of Durango in Mexico while Mexico was involved in a struggle for independence from Spain. To inspire the girls, he told them stories of the great women in history. Juana could envision the female Mexican soldiers as they stood shoulder-to-shoulder with the male soldiers and fought to the death. She learned from the padre that they were called *soldaderas*. In Spain, long before the Conquistadores came to the New World, the soldaderas earned wages for their services. Many battles had been fought with both men and women defending their people and their land. Padre Martinez taught the students about the Iberian settlements along the upper Rio Ebro in the area that became known as Castilla in Spain. From this warrior people came the great Queen Isabella of Spain. They developed a distinct society with its own language, values and customs, which came from their isolation in a harsh land. New Mexico's Hispanic population had the genes and determination to survive under the hardships and hostile conditions it was met with. Isabella had made all men and women where she came from warriors, and all warriors were equal. New Mexico imitated its mother country, Spain. Together with their allies, their Indian neighbors were willing to fight to defend their families and their way of life. Although the Hispanos and the Indians lived and ruled separately, they always came together in times of war to hold on to and defend their way of life.

Juana would never tire of stories about the courageous women of the world. She asked question after question and eagerly waited for answers from the learned priest. "Had Queen Isabella had daughters?" she asked. The padre talked about Isabella's daughter, Catalina de Aragón, who was remembered as one of the most beloved queens in English history. Catalina had ruled England for four years while Henry VIII was away fighting against France. Henry VIII divorced Catalina and sent her back to Spain. Juana wanted to know why Queen Isabella had not protected her. The padre explained that she never saw her daughter's misfortune since she had died before then. The padre also told stories of great male and female pilgrims, including Sylvia of Aquitaine, the great female traveler of the fourth century who had spent her life on a journey to many of the sacred places from Jerusalem, Arabia and Mesopotamia. Sylvia wrote interesting accounts of all her travels. Juana hoped that some day she would be fortunate enough to read the stories of Sylvia of Aquitaine.

Juana also enjoyed the stories of the women who had come to the New World with the Conquistadores. María de Estrada had fought valiantly in Tenochtitlan, along with other women, against the Aztecs for their lives. Both Indian men and women from other tribes had joined in the struggle for freedom from the Aztecs, including La Malinche, the powerful female warrior from Mexico. The Conquistadores wrote, "She fought alongside them as well as any man fighting for their lives and the lives of their comrades." The sixteenth-century Spanish Conquistadora María Velasquez de Cuellar and ten other women had sailed with Pánfilo de Narvaéz to conquer La Florida, and Francesca de Henestrosa had traveled with the de Soto expedition in 1539 disguised as a man. Catalina de Erauso of the seventeenth century also dressed as a man in her long service fighting for the Spanish Empire. The Basque noblewoman received a soldier's pension for her dedication to her king and queen. Juana was saddened by the stories of St. Joan of Arc. Juana asked her teacher, "Why did they have to disguise themselves as men?" The padre explained that the world was not ready to accept women as equals in many ways but that maybe she would someday help to change all that.

Juana was a proud girl, like her Spanish forebears. She was very confident, self-assured and determined. Padre Martinez also taught his students English. Hispano New Mexicans would have to compete with English as a second language since he believed that the sleeping giant to the north would someday influence the territory.

Juana learned how to speak in Tewa from one of the Pueblo Indian servants of the family and to speak French from a French fur trapper who often visited and dealt with her father. It was through her father's dealings with other American immigrants to New Mexico that she also learned other languages and about other cultures around the world. Juana thought it was especially strange that American women could not own property or carry their own maiden surnames once they were married, as was the custom of the Spanish. She was confident in her own identity. Her father had already told Juana, as well as her brothers, how he had divided the land he owned, and she knew when the time came she would be ready to carry on the traditions her parents and all their family before them had passed to her. Many Americans coming into New Mexico were renouncing their American citizenship, pledging allegiance to Mexico, marrying local Hispanic women and inheriting immense properties.

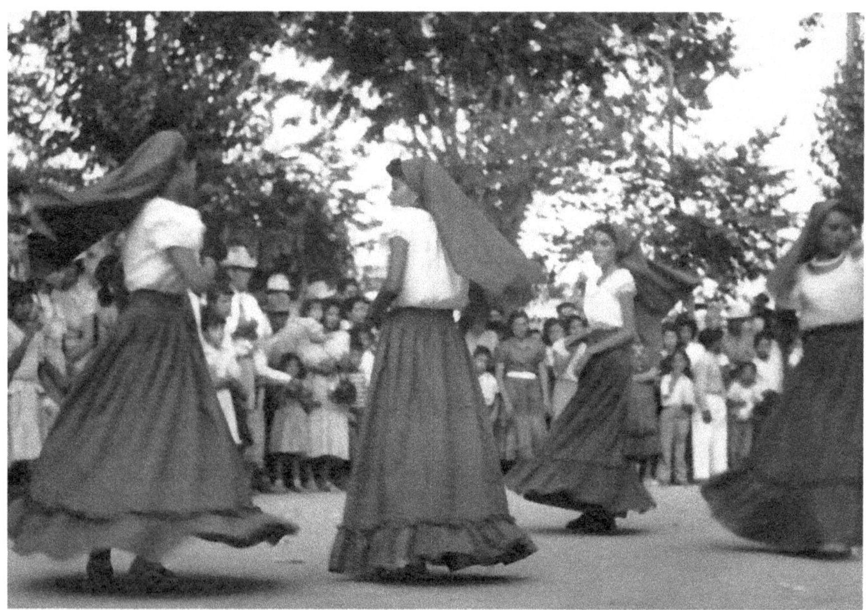

La Raspa, a traditional Spanish colonial dance performed for fiestas in a New Mexico village during the 1930s. *Author's collection.*

The Americans complained about the scandalous behavior of the "Spanish girls." Juana listened one day while shopping for supplies at a local store as some American women talked freely about the condition of the people in the territory. They spoke in English and were certain that no one understood what they were saying. One of them smiled at Juana's mother as she said, "These people practice every vice that can corrupt the human heart and all the qualities that reduce man to the level of a brute."

The other woman responded, "What do our congressmen think they are doing? How is this territory to be annexed to the virtue and intelligence of the American people?"

Another added, "I told my husband, I do not desire to belong to any such union!"

The three women looked at one another and almost in unison proclaimed, "We must demand that something be done about it!"

Juana could not help but intrude by saying, "Did you know that some of us even smoke in public, not in hiding as you do?" The American women walked out of the store stunned.

Back home, her family was getting together to produce molasses with some of the families from Peñasco, as they did every year. The men gathered up the maize cornstalks that didn't have ears and placed them in piles near a designated home. The women, along with their children, removed the leaves, the pikes and the trunk at the bottom. When the men finished their work for the day, and after dinner, they gathered the canes or stalks and took them to where they could produce the syrup or molasses. They placed the canes into a very large dugout cottonwood trunk—sort of what they used to transport water from a clear water system or stream to irrigate their fields. Then, each man used wooden rammers they called *pisones* to mash the cane until it was totally mashed. This was heavy work because it was hard and quick. After it was mashed, the women rapidly placed the resulting liquid to boil in large clay pots that were hung on adobe forms, similar to an oven box where fires were built but with spaces in between for ventilation. The broth or juice would then be placed in hollowed-out barrels that could hold up to fifty gallons. Wooden boards called *bitoques* with cross arrows to create fly presses were then placed on the barrels. A *viga* or beam, measuring twenty-five to thirty feet, was placed over several of these barrels between two holed wooden posts that tied the viga down. They called this the press. Then, some would climb up on the viga and press the cane until the resulting liquid ran into a cottonwood trough that was not used for the animals but solely for this purpose. The women, including Juana, then took the liquid and, once again,

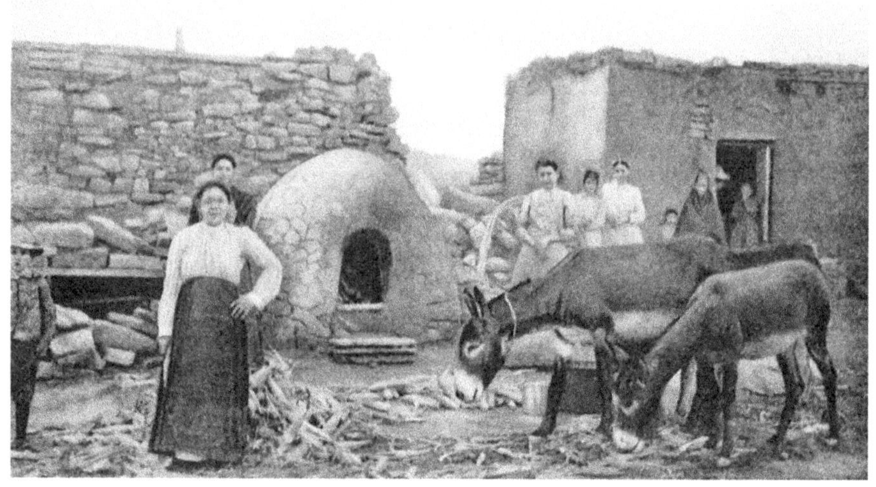

"Sheepranch near Las Vegas, New Mexico," Ed G. Murphey, Real Photo postcard, circa 1911. *Author's collection.*

put it into the clay pots to boil it until the morning, when the molasses or honey-like syrup was ready.

Back in those early days, no one needed money in New Mexico. People throughout the territory farmed, sheepherded, ranched and produced everything for their livelihoods. The rule of the day was to trade for anything else that was needed. In Peñasco, Juana and her family and friends took gallons of the corn syrup and traded it with other New Mexico Hispano families out on the plains, where they would all meet during harvest time. Potatoes, meat, chili, fruit—everything was traded off. When the Hispano families returned home, they had provisions for a year. Juana and her family would travel all the way to the Salt Lakes of Las Salinas and would return home with several hundred-pound gunnysacks of salt to share and trade with their neighbors.

At school, Juana was being recognized as quite a poeta. Juana was a poet, but not a poet in the true sense of the word. In New Mexico, a poet or poeta was someone who was a master at extemporaneous composition of songs, poems, riddles, proverbs—just about anything, even short stories. Padre Martinez was masterful at composing, so he used this as one of his teaching methods. His nephew, Inocencio, the son of his brother Santiago, learned how to play the violin. He made his first violin, which was quite good, by learning the process from a very old violinist and violinmaker in Taos. Juana sang and danced to the sounds of Inocencio's violin.

Juana María Madrid's main interest, over everything else, was to become a famous poeta in New Mexico. She continuously practiced in front of her family at home. A great family outing was to go out and pick piñon nuts. At home, they would clean, salt and roast the piñon and then crack them and eat them while Juana entertained. She was hired at weddings to compose songs that told the life stories of the brides and grooms and how they met to the enjoyment of the entire wedding parties. Once in a while, she threw in a *chiste* (joke) to make everyone laugh and clap in delight. She also had a talent for using her *rebozo*, a black shawl with long fringe, to add tension and mystery to her presentations and performances. The people started affectionately calling her Juana la Marchanta, which was a variation of the word *merchante*, meaning merchant, because they felt she was a merchant with words. Juana Marchanta's fame as a brilliant poeta spread all over the territory of New Mexico. They even heard of her in the San Luis Valley of Colorado.

One day, when Inocencio returned with his uncle Padre Antonio from a trip to Santa Fé, he could hardly wait to tell his friend Juana some great news.

"Juana!" Inocencio yelled out to her when he saw her at school.

"*¿Que quieres?*" she answered.

"*Sabes que*, there's a competition that's taking place in Santa Fé for poetas. I think you can win. The most famous poetas in Nuevo México will be competing. Apolinario Almanzares will be there, and El Zurdo. El doctor Don Juan Bautista y Alarid will give his all against anyone who can challenge him. *¿Que te parece?*"

"*No se*," Juana answered. "I don't think I'm ready."

"Of course you are!" Inocencio exclaimed. "They're giving *ocho cientos reales.* [The equivalent of $100.00, since *ocho reales* was $1.00, *cuatro reales* was $0.50 and *dos reales* was $0.25. In fact, the entire monetary system of the United States was set up under the coinage system of Spain.]" Juana could have made a lot of money during those days if she won. Her parents did not interfere. She was an adult now and could make her own decisions. But they couldn't help but be concerned.

Juana Marchanta decided she would compete. What could she lose? Her reputation as a woman? Her reputation as a Spanish female who spoke out against injustice and held her own against males who felt it was ordained by God that they should be in control? Juana thought about it and decided she had to stand up for her own principles and the rights of women. How could she refuse the challenge?

When Juana Marchanta arrived in Santa Fé, she couldn't believe the commotion on the plaza in front of *El Palacio de los Gobernadores*. The Palace of the Governors was the gathering place of Nuevo México's influential public officials, plus honored and distinguished guests from Mexico City and Missouri in the United States.

The competition began, and the people from Taos were nervous. Padre Martinez gave Juana constant encouragement. With all of the support and encouragement that Juana had, she beat out the competition easily. But then Don Vicente Maestas from El Chamizal, whom they called *Tío Fraile* (the Friar), showed up. Tío Fraile was fierce. He intimidated everyone who came near him, male or female. He lived away from everyone and didn't like people much. He took himself away from his solace every once in a while to show the world what a brilliant mind he had, and he didn't want anyone to forget it. If and when death came, he wanted people to remember and tell stories of him, not just as any mere mortal, but also as a man who equaled the prophetic mind of Nostradamus. He wrapped himself up with a buffalo hide, which they called *concheyos* in New Mexico. He sat near where Juana Marchanta was singing her improvised and beautiful songs.

Juana had never met Tío Fraile, but she knew he was the best there was when it came to the craft of poetas. He, too, had heard of the young woman everyone called Juana Marchanta. He walked up to her and said in a deep voice, "I am Tío Fraile. I have heard some people say you can beat me at my trade. I would like to challenge you with some verses."

"I am very honored, and I accept your challenge," Juana responded.

He said, "*Yo también con mi dinero echo vino a mi garganta, no ando de sinvergüencería como la Juana Marchanta.* [With money I also buy wine for my throat, but I don't go around brazen like Juana Marchanta.]" The famous poet attempted to belittle her with a quick verse.

Juana wasn't about to pass up a good fight, so she answered, "*Por andar de vagamunda, me encontré con el Espantajo.* [For traveling as a vagabond, I shall encounter a scarecrow.]"

As they tested each other, the audience spurred them on. They composed extemporaneous *decimas de amor*. These were verses of unrequited love. Then they came up with *decimas a lo divino*, verses of faith. Finally, they just composed *trabos*, any verse created on the spot when a subject was called out by the audience. Riddles, chistes, dichos and sharp words back and forth—anything was fair game, except bad language. If a foul word was used, then it meant automatic disqualification. Both Juana Marchanta and Tío Fraile were as sharp as whips. But then Juana asked for an answer to a riddle: "*De los muertos salen los vivos; tres eran y cuatro serán. Quiénes son?* [From the dead come the living; there were three and then there will be four. Who are they?]"

Tío Fraile thought and thought, and the audience was perplexed. Finally, Tío Fraile egotistically answered, "It is mankind, of course, because humans never learn."

"No," Juana Marchanta said. "It is the Four Horsemen of the Apocalypse. The Four Horsemen of the Apocalypse: pestilence, war, famine and death. Pestilence subjugates the nations of the world to demonic power. All four

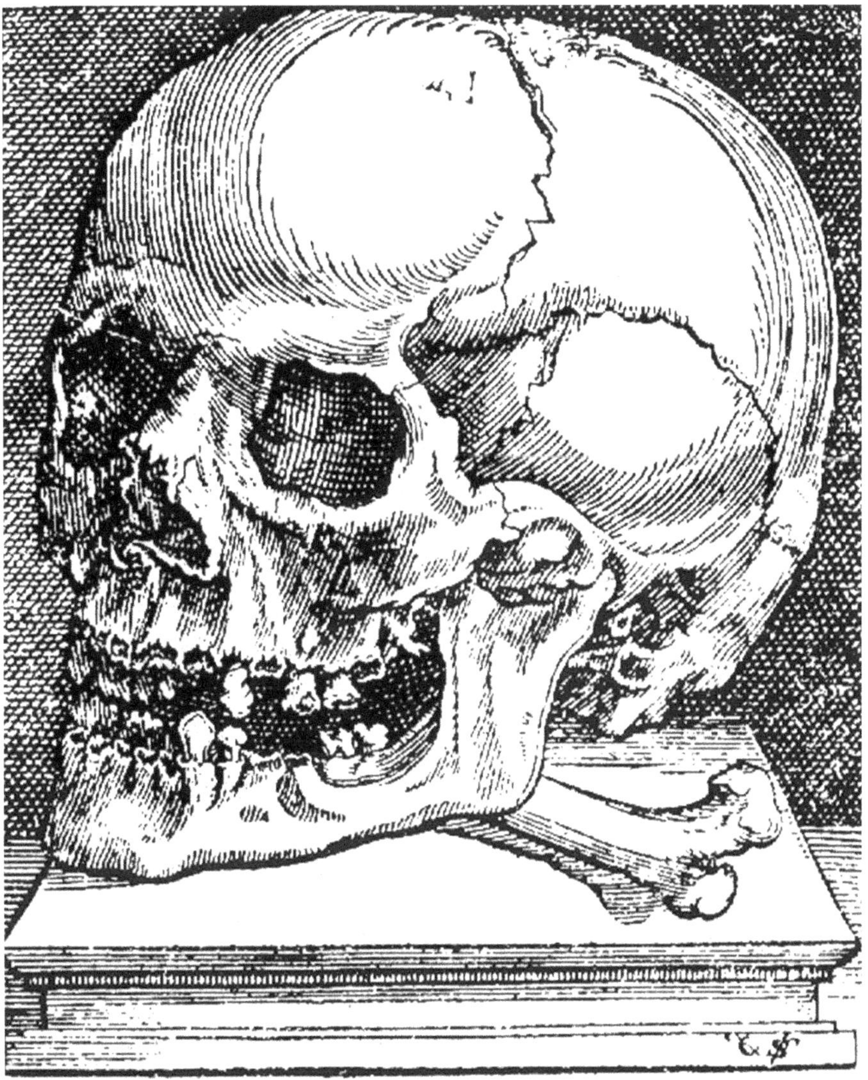

Engraving by Christoffel van Sichem. From *Het Geheele Leven ons Heeren Jesu Christi* (Amsterdam: P.I. Paets, 1648). *Author's collection.*

represent war, domination, death, famine, gluttony and hunger. Death carries remaining souls to their final destinations."

Juana won the contest. As you can well imagine, Vicente Maestas from El Chamizal felt as though someone had taken something from him unfairly. Poor Juana's triumph was short lived. They say that after that night, she disappeared from the face of the earth. Juana Marchanta's family, relatives, friends and even the holy Padre Martinez of Taos searched for her. The search for her lasted for weeks and weeks; even month after month her father, mother, brothers and sisters looked for her. Where could she have gone? What could have happened to her?

They say that one night during a full moon—a quiet, peaceful time—someone was heard singing out in the darkness behind the trees. When they searched, no one was there. Then they heard the faint singing again. One night, someone heard a woman talking out in the hills, laughing, singing and then crying. People in the villages wondered what this was all about. No matter where someone was at night or what time of the night it was, it seemed as though this voice was everywhere. Finally, people came to believe that something very bad happened to Juana Marchanta, but since she had been such a good person in life, she must now be entertaining the angels up in heaven. Like she had always done among the living before, she was making the angels laugh and cry for sheer joy because she was with them.

If you venture out into the hills of Peñasco after the sun has gone down on a quiet and peaceful night, and if you suddenly hear laughter, talking and crying, it may be Juana. You don't need to fear her. It's just her way of showing her excitement at having beaten Don Vicente Maestas, aka Tío Fraile, the best poeta in Nuevo México. The old-timers who still pass down memories of her life call her Juana Marchanta, *La Parpanta* (the Ghost).

## THE SHEEPHERDER AND THE CHUPACABRA

*Oveja que bala, bocado pierde.*
Never let anything distract you from your purpose.

As Francisco looked up at the blue sky, he could see vultures circling above. Once in a while, clouds passing slowly by would cover them, but they were still there. Outspread wings flapping menacingly looked like the wings of devils waiting to swoop down on their victims. The red eyes of the ravenous birds looked down at the helpless prey that meekly looked up from below.

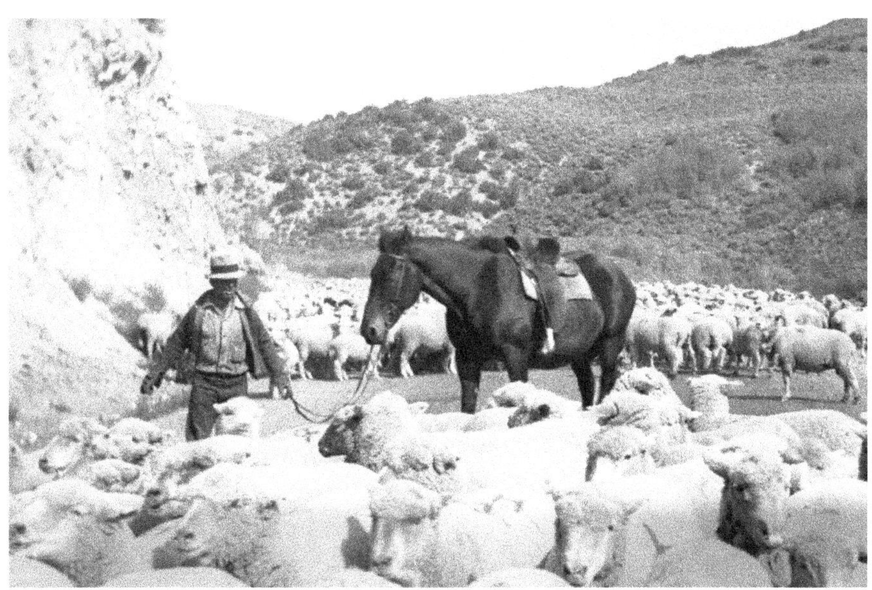

*Above*: "New Mexico Sheepherder," unknown photographer, circa 1940. *Author's collection.*

*Below*: *The Thrashing Machine of New Mexico*. From a sketch by H.W. Elliott, drawn and engraved for the *American Agriculturist*, Wagon Mound, 1870. *Author's collection.*

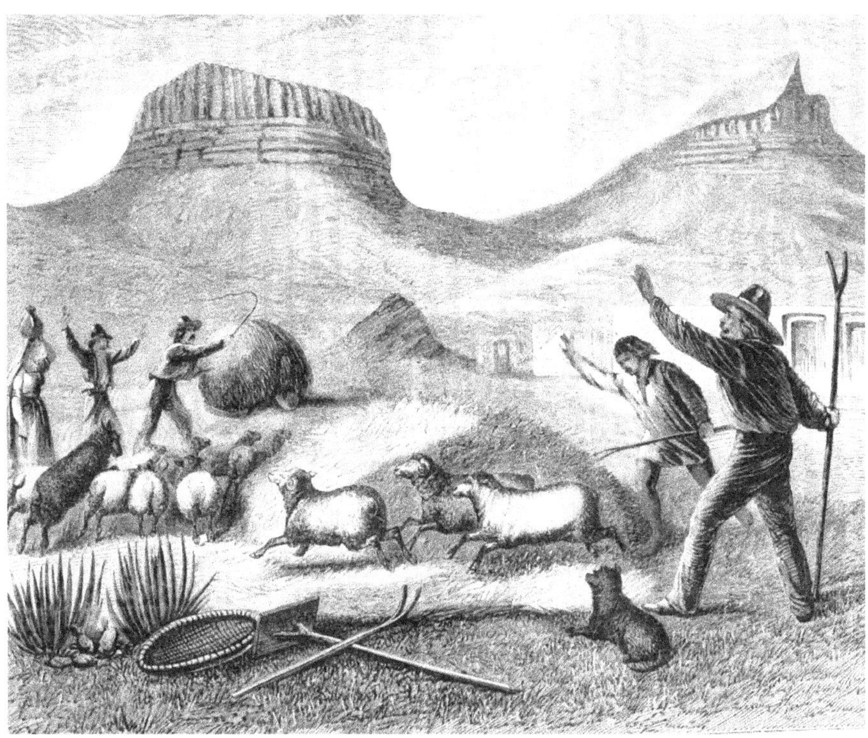

Francisco was the keeper of his flock. He had to protect sheep that were entrusted to him and guide them. Francisco had grown up in a sheepherding family with roots that went back hundreds of years in New Mexico. Ever since his parents and grandparents could remember, sheep had always been important in their family. As a little ten-year-old boy, Francisco had gotten to see the men of his village of Jarales join in and help his father with the sheep shearing. He convinced his father that he could help out, too, so he was given the smallest pair of shears they had, and he learned how to use them. A smiling uncle held the sheep down as the little boy furiously clipped this way and that way, trying to keep up with the older ones.

Francisco Gallegos was small for his age, but his sharp wit made up for it. His dark hair and dark eyes sparkled in the sun, and his skin had darkened since he preferred spending most of his time outdoors. His playtime activities were chopping wood, watering the fields and caring for the farm animals. Francisco would have liked to go to school, but he lived during a time when everyone had to work at home from sunup until sundown just to survive. He did learn how to read and write, so he practiced on his own when he could.

The young sheepherder often played with the sheep dogs, but his favorite companion was his burro, Pánfilo. The burro was an intelligent animal that heehawed like crazy if he thought that his young master was in any kind of danger. Pánfilo was smart, and he could carry a heavy load. Francisco would ride his burro all over the farm, and he would take it with him exploring. The young boy could go great distances on his burro, and one day he decided to go all the way to the *Sierra de los Ladrones* (Thieves Mountain) to look for treasure. A favorite story told around New Mexico was that sometime in 1908, about the time Francisco was born, the Denver Colorado Mint was broken into, and a large amount of gold was stolen. The thieves carted off their loot in wagons and horses and covered their tracks by rubbing the ground with branches. As luck would have it, a windstorm helped their getaway by removing all traces on the dirt. According to the story, the thieves made their way to Las Vegas, New Mexico, and then to nearby Romeroville. A posse had been formed, and it discovered the direction in which the fugitives fled.

When the sheriff's posse arrived in Romeroville, it found a couple of abandoned wagons. It searched the hills but found none of the gold or signs of the outlaws. Old-timers went on to say that the bandits somehow traveled all the way to Sierra de los Ladrones, where they either hid the gold in the caves or buried it in the ground. Thieves Mountain was a popular place for New Mexico outlaws escaping the law. Now called Ladrones Peak, this mountain summit in Socorro County, near La Joya, served as a refuge for marauding Indians during the Spanish colonial days.

Apache and Navajo raiders of the Spanish settlements in the Rio Abajo along the Rio Grande would hide their stolen horses, cattle and sheep there. The steep and treacherous canyons of the mountain served as a safe haven and hideout for outlaws. The infamous Billy the Kid and his gang were supposed to have spent time hiding out at the mountain. It is also claimed that the retreating Spanish hid gold and silver objects from the churches in the caves during the Pueblo Indian Revolt of 1680. Billy the Kid was rumored to have hidden out at Ladrones Peak after his escape from the Lincoln County Jail. He didn't resurface until his pal Billy Wilson delivered a note to him there from his paramour, Paulita Maxwell, who was pregnant with his child. The note said she desperately needed to see him, so Billy rode out of Ladrones into an unsuspected trap and death.

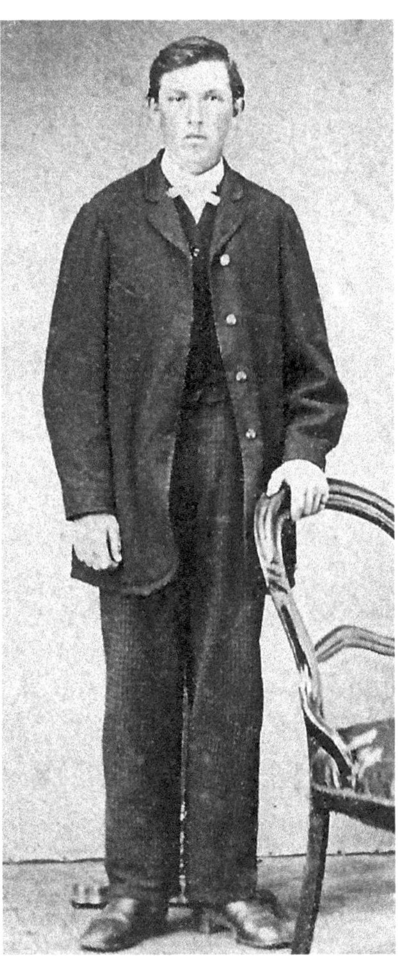

"William H. Bonney, alias Billy the Kid," carte de visite, Harry W. Lucas, photographer, Silver City, New Mexico, circa 1878–80. *Author's collection.*

Young Francisco knew all of the stories and more. He also liked to check things out for himself. It helped to break the monotony of having to watch his flocks of sheep all the time. Francisco was always on the lookout for predators. The vultures circling above reminded him of a wild creature he once saw stalking his flock. It was like nothing he had ever seen before. He had often encountered coyotes, but this one was different. It was like a cross between a coyote and a hyena or even, perhaps, a greyhound and a coyote. It reminded him of a greyhound because it had thick skin that looked hairless. The color was gray and contrasted with its piercing red eyes. Its hind legs were longer than its front legs, so it had a peculiar gait that helped it pounce on the prey. In reality, it even seemed a mutation of the attack dogs that the Spanish Conquistadores had brought with them and the coyote, he thought. After he examined the lifeless bodies of the sheep it had killed, he was shocked to discover they hadn't been eaten. They had only puncture wounds where it seemed that their blood had been drained.

When Francisco talked about his strange encounter with the villagers in Sabinoso, he heard different interpretations of what he saw. One of the men believed he had come across a witches' dog or even a gargoyle because he had seen such an animal pictured in an ancient black book he happened to glimpse by accident. Another felt it had to be a "Devil Dog," which is pretty much the same thing except that this is a transformed devil that has taken on the shape of a dog to attack its victims.

The most interesting story Francisco heard, however, was from Doña Serafina, the old curandera who had just stood by listening without saying a word. She said that many, many years ago, people were finding dead cattle, dead chickens, dead *cibolos* (bison), dead sheep and goats and even a person who seemed like the blood had been drained out. Since whatever it was mainly attacked goats, she said—a goatsucker—the people called the mystery animal a *chupacabra*. Doña Serafina went on to tell them that ancient Indians had this strange breed of animal. She said that she herself had seen one with her own eyes following an Indian witch doctor who had it as a pet. "The chupacabra stopped and stared at me," she said. "It was an evil stare that sent a chill up and down my spine. But I was not going to show it that I was afraid. I just took out my detente, my picture with an embroidered edge that said, '*Detente-el sagrado corazón de Jesús esta conmigo, stop*' [The Sacred Heart of Jesus is with me]. Detentes are to keep evil away from you and protect you. When the chupacabra saw the detente, it gave me a mad stare and followed its master, dragging its long skinny tail and turning to look back at me every now and then. I just held my detente out with my hand toward him. I don't go anywhere without my detente. You never know when you're going to see a chupacabra."

As Francisco sat on a rock remembering Doña Serafinas's words, he took out his own detente of the Sacred Heart of Jesus. It was given to him at his wedding. Even his bride, Cleofas Flores, had received a detente, but hers was the Sacred Heart of Mary. When he was taking his flock out to far pasture, Cleofas said, "Don't forget your detente." She had tears in her eyes knowing she would not see him for months.

Francisco left on his journey in search of good green pasture for his sheep. It had been more than a day since he had found an *ojo* in an arroyo, a spring that offered sweet and refreshing water for him and his flock. Springs of water that would suddenly appear between rocks, crannies and in arroyos saved many lives along the Camino Real. The Indians and many of the old-timers knew where the ojos were. Francisco had been more concerned with finding wild grass for his sheep to eat, and now he had a dozen or more lambs to worry about. He was sure he would find water somewhere. He knew the old methods that had been passed down by his Spanish forefathers included keeping an eye out for birds flying out of a certain area. Birds, even vultures, knew where water was. Besides, it seemed like there might even be a desert rainstorm since storm clouds were brewing. Francisco rushed his flock away from an area near the Rio Puerco, a dry riverbed prone to devastating runoff, to seek a safe haven.

In the distance, Francisco saw what appeared to be a tower and some buildings. When he finally got there with his flock, he discovered that it was the ruins of an early Spanish colonial village, along with what remained of a torreon. The torreon was an architectural form that dated back to the Iberian and Roman periods of ancient Spain. The history of the torreon went as far back as two thousand years, and it had a wide use throughout New Mexico as protection against wild animals or attacking Indians.

On this particular day, and on this late afternoon, Francisco had been unable to find water for his thirsty sheep. He saw an ancient willow tree, so he cut a forked branch from it to fashion a divining rod. Francisco knew that all of the early water wells his ancestors had dug were found this way. As he walked around lightly holding the tips of the forked branch, it suddenly turned downward. He got his small shovel from his mule and started to dig. The dirt was hard and dry. After painstakingly digging down for about four feet, Francisco finally gave up when he lost his energy. Although the sand underneath was a little moist, he had no idea how far down he would have to dig to find water. He decided to wait until the following day to track down water.

After the young sheepherder set up camp, he cooked some dry green chili and beef jerky in a little water. It was a delicious meal. Normally, he would have slaughtered and cooked a lamb, but this was mostly done when two or three sheepherders would get together to socialize and share a meal. Around dusk, when Francisco was eating, he heard a strange sound coming from a ridge. He looked, but nothing was there. Then suddenly, his sheep began to bleat uncontrollably. A strange creature just outside the ring, sniffing and giving the shepherd a mad stare, had disturbed them. It was a chupacabra, and it hungrily looked around at the scared sheep. Francisco took his détente out of his shirt pocket, and while holding it in his hand, he recited the Lord's Prayer several times in succession. The chupacabra looked at him with its red eyes and growled fiercely, then turned and walked away. His détente had saved his life.

The next day, Francisco found plenty of water and grass for his sheep. He returned home to his family and told them of his adventures with the chupacabra.

## HALF PAST TWELVE

*El que anda de noche con cualquier bulto se espanta.*
He who is out at night is easily frightened.

Andres Segura and Moises Lujan were good friends. They went to Our Lady of Sorrows Catholic School, which was near the Old Town Plaza in Las Vegas. The park in the plaza was the scene of many hangings back in the Old West. It is claimed that some of the ghosts of the poor devils who were hanged at the plaza appeared each night, moaning and groaning about their misdeeds. The old nuns who ran the school were pretty strict. They reminded the children about the consequences of sinful ways and that they themselves could end up like those lost souls. They told the kids to keep away from the Gallinas River, which was nearby; not to go near the cemetery on the hill; and to beware of dark strangers. Andres and Moises went anyway.

The two rough-and-tough boys loved to go to the Billiard Palace on the east side of the river on Friday nights. The palace was at least three or four miles away, but to them it didn't matter; they enjoyed going there. The two boys also liked to play pranks. One day, they waited impatiently behind a building for the old hermit who lived in a cave at Hermit's Peak to come into town. The hermit would go into Las Vegas once a month to buy beans, dried meat and hard tack biscuits. Once in a while, he'd buy hard candy or *piloncillo* as his treat. As the hermit rounded the corner of the building dressed in his long gray robe and hood, walking with a staff, the boys jumped out and yelled. They scared the daylights out of the old guy. "I'll get you *malcriados*!" the hermit yelled out, raising his fist as the two scampered away. Oh, it was great fun for Andres and Moises, but everyone has to pay their dues. They used to say in the old days, "What goes around comes around." One day, it certainly did.

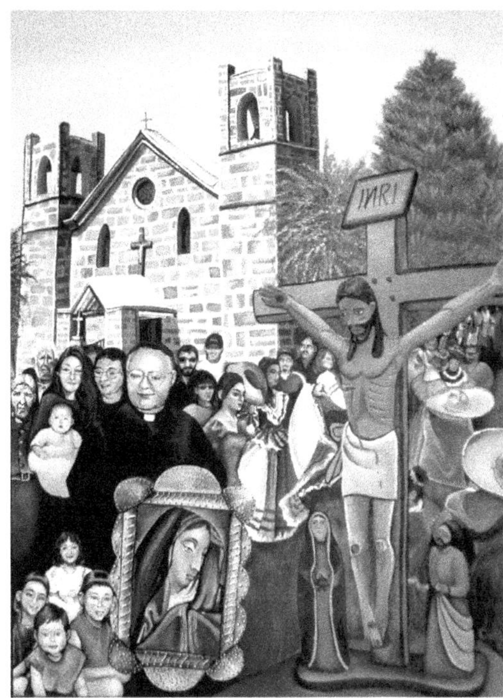


*Nuestra Señora de Los Dolores de Las Vegas*, acrylic on canvas painting. *©1998 Rosa María Calles, Los Lunas Museum of Heritage and Arts collection.*

It was a bright sunny Friday morning when Andres and Moises got together at their usual meeting place down by the plaza. They decided to ditch school and spend the day exploring and having fun. The boys first took a hike up to El Crestón Hill, traveling through the gulley and the arroyos. They went all the way to the old Mount Calvary Cemetery, where they sat on the tombstones and checked out the graves. At the end of the day, they traveled to the Billiard Palace, where they spent hours playing pool. It was quite dark when they finally decided to head back home.

On the way home, they joked and laughed about firing rocks with their slingshots at the birds and bullying some of the little boys at school. The mischievous boys crossed the bridge over the Gallinas River into Old Town. They hadn't noticed it was a darker night than usual until they got near the Kiva Theater, where silent films were shown. *Dracula* with Bella Lugosi was the main feature. Since it was late, the theater had already closed for the day. As they walked by, they noticed an old woman standing near a building leaning on a cane. She had long white hair, a black-fringed shawl and a black dress.

"What time is it, boys?" she asked as they walked by.

Andres looked at his make-believe watch and answered, laughing, "It's half past twelve, old lady."

"Don't you think it's time you both should be home in bed?" she asked.

Andres and Moises snickered and kept on walking. They began to feel uneasy. At times, they heard footsteps as if someone were following close by, so every now and then they would look back, but there was no one there. Neither boy spoke about his fear, not wanting the other to think he was scared. After all, they had a reputation to uphold. Instinctively, they both walked faster up the forbidding road. For some reason, the old woman's stare had frightened them. Finally, Moises broke the silence by asking Andres, "Don't you think the old lady was kind of weird?"

Andres, not eager to answer, said, "Yeah, what business is it of hers to ask why we're not in bed?"

As the two boys rounded the corner of the Romero Mercantile Building, they felt more comfortable, so they slowed down their pace. Andres' and Moises's mouths fell open. There stood the old woman next to the building, leaning on her cane. She asked them, "What time did you boys say it was?"

Now they were frightened, and they didn't care to pretend they were brave. They ran so fast it seemed as if their feet didn't even touch the ground. There was no way on earth the old woman could have gotten there before them. Without thinking or saying a word, each one took off in a different direction. It was each man for himself. Besides, this was a life and death situation. This was no time to be a hero. Moises ran up the hill toward his home. Andres yelled as he tripped and fell to the hard ground. Moises didn't stop; he just kept running. Andres looked at the old woman as she moved toward him. Like a crazy person, he picked himself up quickly and screamed all the way home. Dogs began to bark, which added to his dilemma.

The lights went on at his home as he neared the house. His father came out to see what was wrong with his panic-stricken son. Andres yelled out, "Someone's chasing me!"

"There's no one there, *hijo*," his father said.

Andres immediately became silent. He looked around. There wasn't anyone there. He quietly entered his home as his father laughed and teased him. Then, sternly, his father added, "By the way, son, we've got some talking to do. Sister Frances Borgia contacted me today. Apparently, you weren't at school, so you've got some explaining to do. For now, go to your room, where you should have been in the first place! Remember, son, what goes around comes around."

They say everyone was really surprised at the transformation the boys went through after that night. They would get up very early and go to school and stay in school. They never bullied anyone again. They even helped the nuns with chores. But do you know what the biggest change for Andres and Moises was? They were never, ever out again after the sun went down. They were scared to death of the dark, being out on the town at night and, most of all, ghostly strangers.

## A Dark, Misty Night

*El que no muere, se vuelve ver.*
He who does not die is seen again.

The warm, lazy sun was barely rising behind the green piñon tree–filled hills that surrounded the deep valley of San Isidro del Rio Pecos when Antonio Lopez got up. It was the start of a new day, but he could hardly wait for nightfall to come. His mother had said it was OK for him to go to the Saturday night dance, and his father was letting him use the car. Antonio took out his best shirt and pants from the closet and polished his boots. Then he washed and waxed his father's red and white '56 Chevy and cleaned up the leather interior of the car.

The dance would begin at nine o'clock. Antonio helped his dad with work that needed to be done, and the hours went by too quickly. He was running late. He rushed to eat and take a bath and was finally on his way out the door. "I'm leaving, *mama*!" he yelled as he rushed out the door.

"You better be home before twelve," she responded.

His mother went to the door and said to Antonio as he got into his car, "*Acuérdate, hijo, sal de la casa y cuenta lo que te pasa. Ten cuidado* [Remember, son, if you are not careful, you may come home telling stories of things you didn't want to tell]." He laughed and drove off on the dirt road.

It was a dark, misty night as Antonio drove along the narrow, winding road. Soon, he turned onto the main highway that would take him to Ribera, twenty-five miles away. Only the front headlights of the car were visible as the light coming from them showed him the way on the lonely stretch of road. Antonio would have liked to listen to music, but the car radio had not worked for some time, and nothing his father did to fix it had made a difference.

Antonio thought of the dance, his friends and which girls would probably be there. Suddenly, his headlights illuminated someone in the middle of the road standing directly in front of his car. He swerved the car to avoid hitting the person and came to a stop right next to whoever it was. Antonio leaned over and lowered the passenger's window. "Are you OK…do you need some help?" he nervously asked.

It was a girl with long brown hair. She turned, looked at him and answered, "Yes."

"Do you need a ride somewhere?" Antonio asked.

"Yes. Ribera," she replied.

"I am on my way there, too," Antonio told her.

Without answering, she opened the door, sat down and closed it. Surprised, Antonio didn't know what to say; he just took his foot off the brake and continued to drive down the road.

Antonio's heart pounded hard as the beautiful stranger looked straight ahead. She turned toward him at one point, and he caught a glimpse of her bright green eyes before she turned away again. He tried to start up a conversation, but she nervously began playing with a large locket pinned to a white lace bow attached to her dark blue dress with long, ruffled sleeves. Antonio decided he would wait for her to speak before he said anything else. In the meantime, he would quietly enjoy the company of his mysterious silent stranger.

"We are almost in Ribera. Where is it that you would like for me to take you?" Antonio asked.

"La Palma," she answered.

Amazed, Antonio told her, "I'm going there, too! The Purple Blues are playing tonight. Everyone will be there."

It was teens' night, and the Purple Blues was a popular dance band. He thought to himself, "What more could a guy want? Life is great." The young girl's expression did not change.

Antonio parked the Chevy, stepped out of the car and rushed over to open the door for his lovely new friend. The couple walked quickly into the ballroom, where the band had already started playing a northern New Mexican *ranchera*. The ballroom was a large dance hall decorated with purple and white crepe paper streamers. The band was up on a stage that was dimly lit with blue lights.

Antonio saw his friends standing against the wall at the darkened corner opposite the entrance. He knew José and the rest of his friends would be anxious to meet the girl he was with. When he saw his best friend, José, start walking toward them, he immediately asked his companion to dance with him. She didn't say anything. She walked with him to the dance floor. Antonio did not want to give José a chance at dancing with his new friend. José was quite popular with the girls, and he enjoyed

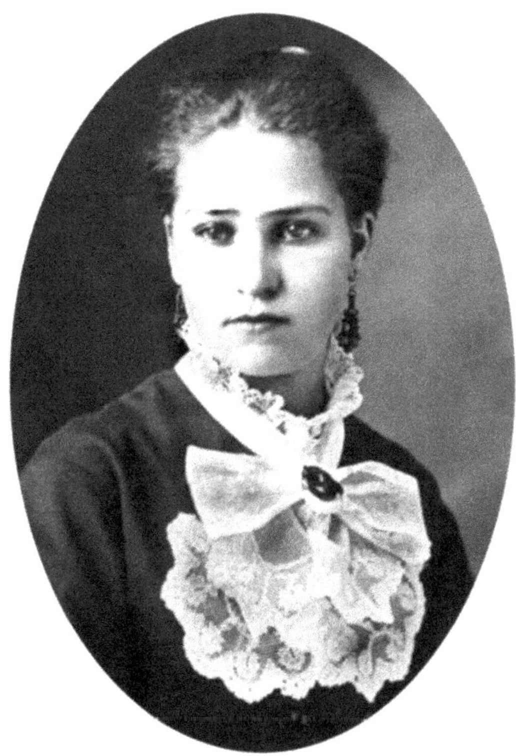

Carte des visite, circa 1850.
*Author's collection.*

laughing at his friends after taking away their dance partners. José stood there looking surprised.

Antonio and his dance partner moved rhythmically to the music, forgetting anyone else was present. She danced as if in a trance, mesmerizing Antonio. For the first time, she was smiling, and her smile was spellbinding. He could not stop dancing. He held on to her and didn't want to let go. The band, too, felt compelled to play continuously and did not stop until midnight. José and his friends watched curiously from a distance.

Antonio and his captivating new friend came to an abrupt stop as the entrancing music of the band also stopped at the stroke of midnight. The young woman's smile disappeared, and she now seemed sad. She did not speak but began walking toward the door. Antonio offered to take her home. She accepted the invitation. She sat quietly on their way back. He noticed a tear roll down her cheek. "Is something wrong?" he asked.

She didn't answer.

They neared the place where he had picked her up. "Where should I go from here? Antonio asked.

"I do not live very far," she replied. "I'll walk home from here."

She was trembling. He reached into the back seat. "Here, please take my jacket. It's cold."

She took the jacket and put it on. "*Gracias*," she said. She opened the door, moved out slowly, closed it lightly and silently walked away into the night.

Antonio sat there motionless as he saw the bewitching young woman disappear between the pine trees. He thought, "I don't even know what her name is. How could I have been so dumb?" He began to speak out loud to himself. "I don't even know where she lives. I don't know anything about her. How in the world could I have been so stupid?"

Antonio got back home at one o'clock in the morning, snuck into his room and went straight to bed, but he couldn't sleep. He just tossed and turned thinking about the girl, the dance and everything that had happened that evening. He finally came up with an idea. "I'll just go back to where I picked her up and search for her house. I'll use the excuse that I went to pick up my jacket and then talk to her. Anyway, she really seemed to like me a lot," he thought.

The next day, he got up early. He borrowed the car from his parents again. "I've got to get some information from my friends on a project we are doing at school," he lied.

"All right, but come right back," his parents ordered.

Antonio had chosen to lie to his mother and father. He couldn't help himself. He drove to the exact spot where he had first seen the girl. He got out of the car and followed her trail between the pine trees. He walked and walked, but he found no house. He hiked up a hill and stopped to look around. Searching across the valley, he noticed a very old adobe house that was barely visible. "Could that be her home?" he wondered. He went to the house.

It took a while to walk all that way, but Antonio finally got there. He walked up the steps and knocked on the old screen door. A moment later, an elderly woman with a smile on her face opened the door. "*Buenos días, hijo*, how may I help you?" she politely greeted him. In spite of the old woman's friendly greeting, Antonio felt uneasy. There was something about her eyes that scared him. They were very large and pale blue, and her stare was penetrating.

Antonio nervously responded, "I met a young girl last night. It was cold, and I lent her my jacket. Does she live here?"

"I'm the only one that lives here," she told him.

"Are there any other houses nearby where she might live?" he asked.

"No other houses for miles," she answered.

"She must live around here somewhere," Antonio countered.

Suddenly, there was a loud noise coming from inside. The old woman quickly turned. "Now what are you up to? You behave yourself!" she shouted. A small monkey flew through the air and landed in her arms. "Are you showing off for our guest?" She turned to Antonio and invited him in. Antonio did not really want to enter, but she insisted.

The front room was even stranger than the old woman. There were shelves against the walls with many jars filled with different kinds of concoctions and herbs hanging from a wall. Against another wall was a large wood stove with a black kettle on it. In a corner of the room was a fenced-in area, and inside was a large pig grunting and looking at Antonio. The woman pulled out a chair and had Antonio sit as she asked, "Who are you looking for?"

He said, "I don't know her name, but she has light green eyes and dark brown hair. She wore a dark blue dress with long ruffled sleeves and a large locket that was pinned to a white lace bow on the front of her dress."

"The girl you're describing is María Lucia Dominguez," the old woman said, surprised.

Antonio asked excitedly, "Is she here? Can I see her? I would really like to talk to her."

"That would be impossible," the woman said emphatically. "She's been dead for many, many years!"

"You must be mistaken," he said.

"Follow me."

Antonio followed the woman as she started walking up a path. They had only walked a short distance when they saw a cross hidden among the trees. The old woman walked over to the cross and told him, "This is where she is buried."

As he looked at the cross, he saw that his jacket was lying on top of the grave. "Did you put it there?" Antonio shouted, "Is this a joke?"

"Now, now, young man, calm down. You aren't the first stranger to come to my door asking to see her. She occasionally decides to join the living, especially to dance. I must return to my warm house. I can't take the cold like you young people." Then the old woman disappeared.

Antonio stood there in total shock. It was like a nightmare. But then he thought that there had to be an explanation. He noticed the name María Lucia Dominguez with the date 1883 inscribed on the cross and the words, "*Que descanse en paz* [May she rest in peace]." He nervously picked up his jacket and slowly walked away. Every now and then, he would glance over his shoulder as he walked to his car.

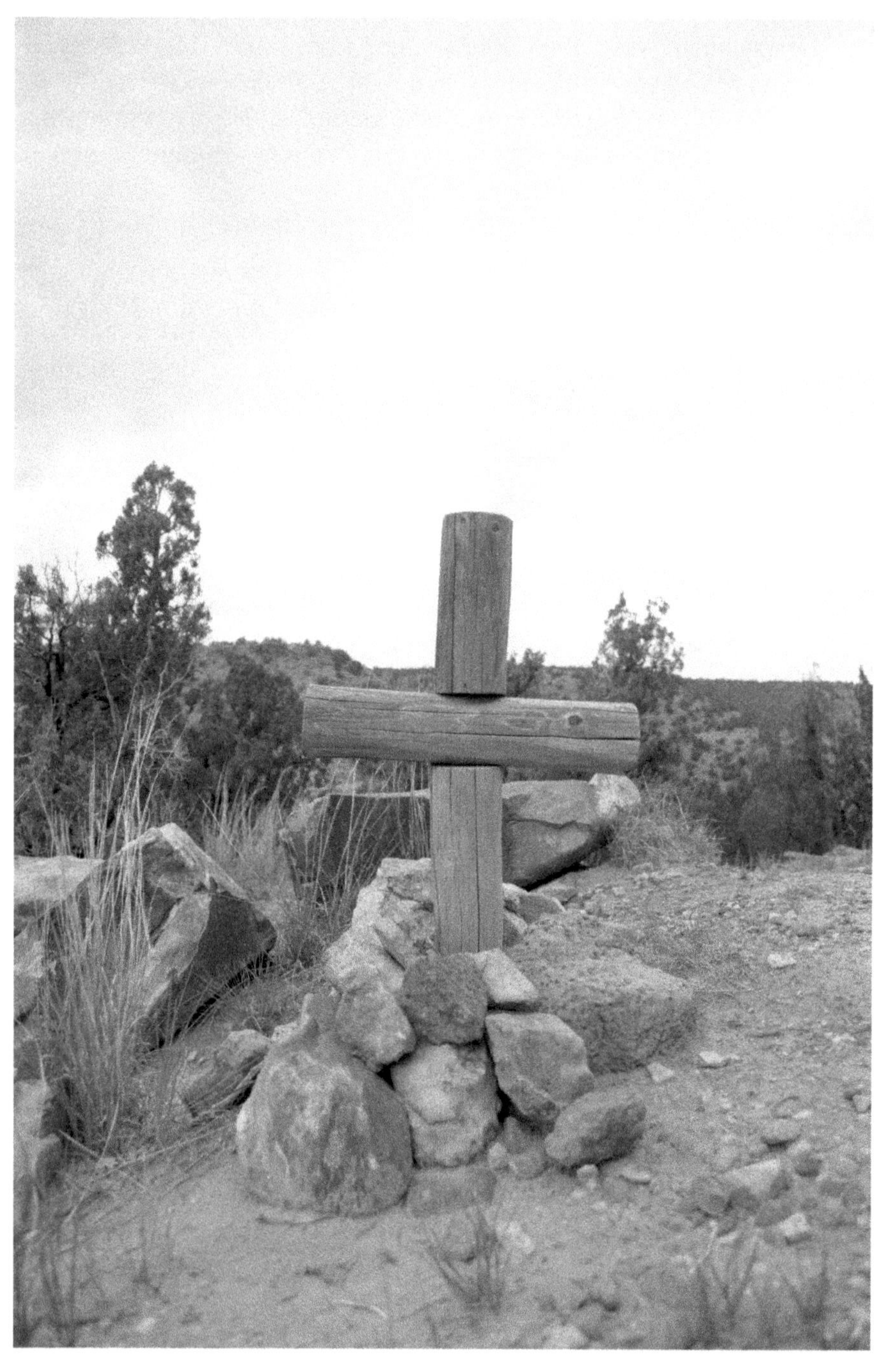

"Cross," photograph. *©2010 Ramon Juan Carlos de Aragón.*

He was startled when he saw an owl standing directly in front of him. He remembered what his grandmother had once told him. "*Hijito, no le tengas miedo a los tecolotes* [don't be afraid of owls]; that is, unless one blocks your path, because that is an omen that something bad will happen." Antonio began to run to get away from the owl and didn't stop until he got into his car. He started the car, and the radio turned on at the same time. The radio now played the song he and María had last danced to. He tried to turn the radio off, but the knob was broken. He gave up messing with the radio and quickly drove back home.

Antonio thought, "I was there. I touched her. I didn't imagine it."

The sun was already setting when he got home. He reached for his jacket and held it in his hands. Antonio put the jacket on and automatically put his hands into his pockets. He touched something. It was cold. He pulled it out. It was María's locket. He looked at the old locket and pressed the edge, and it sprung open. His heart raced as he saw two painted pictures inside. On the right side was the girl he had met the night before. On the left was a picture of…him? But he had never met this girl before. How could his picture be in her locket next to hers and with the clothes he had worn to the dance? It wasn't possible, and yet there it was. He couldn't sleep unless he kept a candle lit in his room from then on.

Antonio never married. He was a good son and took care of his parents until their deaths. He lived his entire life in the little valley of San Isidro del Rio Pecos. The townspeople say he never stopped talking about the beautiful girl with the bright green eyes in the dark blue dress. He returned to the home of the old woman, but even that was a mystery. It was in ruins. Some said the woman who had lived there long ago was a witch, and no one really knew what happened to her or where she went.

Antonio bought the land. The people of Pecos remembered him long after his death. They say he was a very good man with a big heart who loved planting flowers. Every chance he had, he would purchase more seed for flowers. They would tell him he had bought enough seed to cover the whole town in flowers. He would smile and say they were for the woman with the green eyes. He told people close to him that on the day he died, he wanted to be buried in the land where he had last seen her.

Upon his death, the people processed with his body to bury him near the pine trees he loved so much. To their amazement, the earth near the pine trees was covered in flowers in every direction as far as the eyes could see, and in the center of it all was a cross inscribed with the name María Lucia Dominguez, the most beautiful woman who ever lived.

## ANGELINA CHÁVEZ

*Doña Sebastiana es doña de maña.*
Death always finds a way.

The pressures of the day began to fill my mind with senseless idle thoughts. I stood near the entrance, unnoticed and alone. I saw my sister Elena in a corner of the room talking to several people. She was pointing to the small of her back as if telling them about another of her imaginary pains. She was certain she also had my father's terminal illness. Elena had become a hopeless hypochondriac after her husband left her. Other men about town found her attractive, but she would remain aloof, thinking everyone was beneath her. I needed to leave. I knew they were too busy to notice that I was gone.

I was almost out of the room. I thought I could escape, but Elena called, "Hey, Antonio, where are you going?"

"I'm pretty tired," I said. "I think I'll go lie down for a while."

"Poor guy!" José added. My older brother José desperately needed someone to look down on, so I was always the one he picked on. He prided himself on being the life of any gathering. His wife, Alicia, took up where he would leave off.

I heard the sound of laughter as I walked up the winding stairway to the bedroom. It added to the sense of loneliness that was building up inside of me. My father had been a realist, living his life one day at a time. I wish I could have been more like him. In my father's old papers and photographs, I was certain I would find the key to the many questions I had about his past. They were mine now.

I pulled out an old metal box from beneath my bed and studied a picture of Angelina Chávez. Angelina was my father's first wife. She died after they had been married for two years. Her first husband was Joaquin Chávez. He was much older than Angelina, and they said he died of a heart attack. The photo showed a young girl with a pleasant smile. In my room, I had other mementos of the Chávezes' past. Paintings hung on the walls that had been done by Joaquin Chávez's sister, Emma. The paintings had an eerie quality since they were portraits of the straight-laced Chávez family. I especially liked the beautiful gold-leaf frames that housed them. My mother had often wanted to get rid of any vestige of Angelina Chávez, but I pleaded with her to let me have the mementos. The room I slept in was said to have been the one in which Joaquin

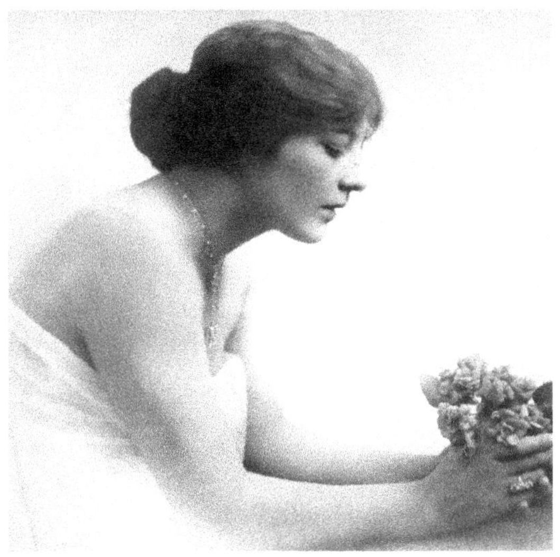

"Prima Donna," photo by C. Floyd Coleman, Gould & Marsden Studios, New York, 1922. *Author's collection.*

Chávez died. The box contained the only remaining photo of Joaquin Chávez. It was taken while he was sitting in his study contemplating the fire in the fireplace. It was clear he had been a tall, thin man with a ghostly complexion.

A knock at my door broke the silence. I got up and walked to open it. My mother was standing there still wearing her black dress and jacket. I asked her right away, "Mother, do you know anything about what happened to Angelina Chávez?"

She answered, "The only thing they said was that she died from a ruptured appendix. Your father never told me anything. He was always secretive about his past. We shouldn't tamper with anything we don't understand. I have to get back to our guests. Please come down soon." Then she walked away.

We lived in a two-story Victorian house. From the balcony on the second floor, one could see the buildings on the plaza. Joaquin Chávez built the house as a wedding gift for his bride. Chávez was the son of early immigrants. He was both a perplexing and mysterious man. People would recount legends about the appearance of Chávez's ghost. Many would swear they could hear unearthly crying and screams coming from inside the walls. Manuel Alvarado, my father, became the owner of the Chávez house through his marriage with Angelina.

"Antonio, hurry up and open the door! I've been knocking loud enough to wake the dead!" my sister hollered. "Everyone is asking for you. You aren't happy unless you see Mother sick. You don't help us with anything. You're

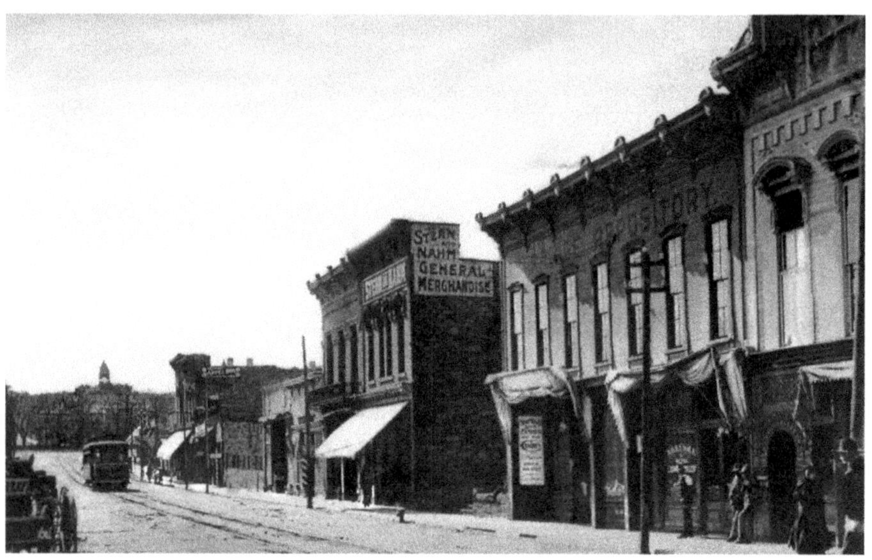


Bridge Street (showing Plaza Park on the west side), Las Vegas, New Mexico, tinted postcard, C.L. Mann-Baily, Importer and Publisher, Las Vegas, New Mexico, circa 1908. *Author's collection.*

only concern is with yourself and what you can get away with. She wants you to join us."

I took my time walking down the stairs. José questioned me when I arrived in the dining room. "What were you doing? Sleeping?"

Alicia, more concerned with the food on the table, managed a remark. "Oh, José, leave him alone. He's harmless. Let's eat, the food is getting cold."

I had already blocked out every word I heard from my mind. My brother spoke again. "Antonio, why didn't you ever help Father with the business instead of toying with your ideas?"

Everyone turned to look at me. I was embarrassed, so I stayed quiet. Everything was so unpleasant for me. I glanced around at the others present. My life was filled with distressing emotions. Finally, people began to leave. The agony would resume in the morning. The funeral was scheduled for nine o'clock.

Death, anybody's death, is like an unwanted dream. But to me, my father's death was a nightmare. I couldn't understand why my father no longer wished to live. It seemed to me he had never stopped loving his first wife. He talked very little about her, but her memory continued to touch everyone's lives. The reality of it all was nothing now but a distant memory. The thoughts that crossed my mind filled me with disgust. The sight of my father's burial covered me with contempt for those who had gathered to join us. They reminded me of insect-like vermin, with clutching, grasping tentacles. I stared hard at the wooden coffin that now held my father's cold body, reliving memories of days gone forever. The crying mixed with the priest's mumbled eulogy set the stage for a drama of changing scenes within my mind. The priest's final words faintly reached me: "*Requiem eternam dona ei, Domine, et lux perpetua leceat ei*, Amen. May his soul rest in peace and reach eternal salvation."

As the seconds ticked by, I was too involved with my recollections to notice that the crowd was steadily moving toward me. As the people drew near to offer condolences, my deep thoughts were broken. "I'm very sorry, hijo, but maybe it was for the best. He was getting on in years, you know."

One voice emerged above the others. It had a force beneath it. "I'm so sorry. Well, it did have to happen sooner or later. I hope that you can accept that."

At long last, the customary ritual was over. Storm clouds gathered as we got ready to leave. The thunder roared like a lion, and the lightning shot out menacingly. Everyone had to enter his or her dull, black limousine. The funeral dirge could be heard as people moved slowly to their cars.

A crisp, cold breeze whipped my hair, and I felt it moving on my face. The dark sky was swollen with rain-filled clouds. I felt like the air was oppressive, and I struggled to breathe. The large monument stones and crosses of nearby tombs loomed high as sentinels of the dead in the cemetery. Towering over all the rest was my father's black cross. I looked away as my mother's cry called for my attention. I looked back at the cross, but it was not there. Was it a vision of what was to come? Was it my cross? My mood was one of disillusion and bitterness. My heart had searched for answers to so many questions. Now my only link to the truth was gone.

The reception followed at our home. As people waited to enter, I helped my mother walk in. She immediately became the center of everyone's attention. This was something she had never experienced as my father's second wife. It fitted her well, and she liked every minute of it.

My duty was done. José and Elena relished all the attention. I wanted none of it. In my depression, I found a space to sit, and I recalled my father's last night. Had I been dreaming or really experiencing something so disturbing? That night at the hospital, I was overcome with fear. I was certain of some power within the room where my father rested that I could not understand. My father became agitated. His face had

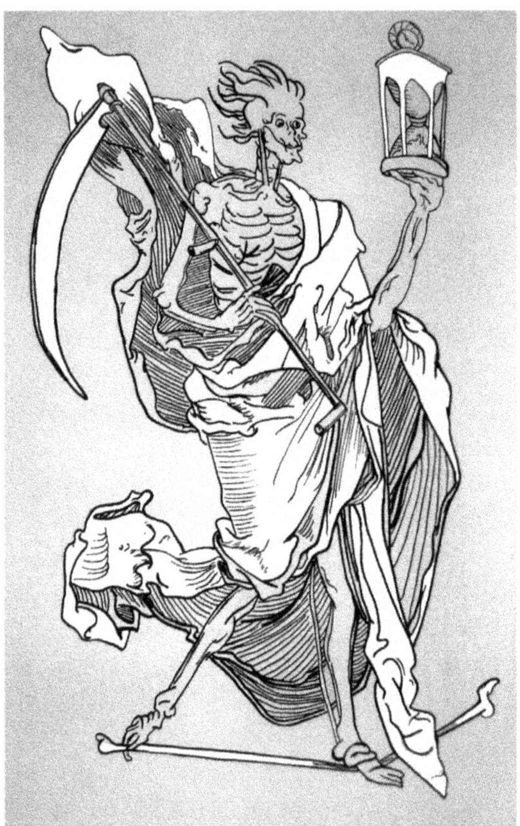

*Angel of Death*, pen-and-ink drawing. *Courtesy Rosa María Calles.*

gone through a sharp series of changes. A face of pain-filled agony was altered into one of despair. He was no longer the powerful man who had influenced so many people. His features were those of a man spent. His thin, hard lips could no longer form commands. His teeth gripped with a crack, and his clenched knuckles projected a final struggle. At times, he seemed to speak, but to whom? His eyes had a distant stare that never rested on me.

There was an uneasy silence that filled the bedroom where my father lay on his deathbed. The silence was broken when he suddenly jolted in fear and cried out, "My God, please help me!" I realized we were not alone as I held his hand. The doorknob turned. The door opened a few inches, and I could only see darkness. My father started tossing violently, repeating, "No, no, no!" The words echoed endlessly through my mind.

My first impulse was to close the door, so I pushed it shut and leaned a chair against it. A minute later, the door shook violently, and the chair came crashing down. Once again, there was only darkness on the other side of the open door. I couldn't understand what was happening. I thought I was going mad. Then, the form of a woman appeared at the doorway. I was petrified. I felt that to her I was not present. With eyes fixed on my father, she reached out for him. He released my hand and closed his eyes. He was gone.

The spirit of Angelina Chávez had returned and taken her beloved.

# ABOUT THE AUTHOR

Ray John de Aragón was born on January 19, 1946, in Las Vegas, New Mexico. His great-grandmother Dona Catalina Mondragon de Valdez, who was a curandera, a medicine woman, delivered him. He grew up with the culture, traditions, heritage and the history of Spanish New Mexico, which dates back to the settlement of the territory by Spanish colonists in 1598. His background is steeped in the folkloric mystery and intrigue that was passed down in his family for generations. His upbringing included listening to centuries-old stories of ghosts, witches and holy spirits that traverse the dark hours of the night. Because of his past history, Ray John de Aragón traveled as a storyteller, thrilling audiences with tales of terror and suspense. Ray John's first university degrees were in education. His advanced degrees are in American studies with an emphasis on the Spanish history, customs and language of New Mexico. He is an internationally recognized author with several published books. He is also a recognized visual artist and *santero*, a maker of religious images.

www.ingramcontent.com/pod-product-compliance
Lightning Source LLC
LaVergne TN
LVHW060933110826
845147LV00030B/1159

* 9 7 8 1 6 0 9 4 9 5 7 2 5 *